The Crete Walking Society

Richard Clark

Praise for Richard Clark's Books

'Clark is particularly good on the colours, flavours and scents of Greece. He has got under the skin of the place in a way few outsiders have been able to.'

Mark Hudson, winner of the Somerset Maugham Award, the Thomas Cook Travel Book Award and the Samuel Johnson Prize

'Richard Clark captures the spirit of the Greece I love. I long to see the places he describes.'

Jennifer Barclay, author of *Falling in Honey, An Octopus in My Ouzo* and *Wild Abandon*

'There is poetry in Richard Clark's words and through his eyes. I recommend anyone missing Greece, visiting Greece or just wishing they could go to Greece to take a look!'

Sara Alexi, author of *The Greek Village Series*

'Thanks, Richard, for adding your great eye to your gifted pen in service to sharing the essence of Greece with the world!'

Jeffrey Siger, bestselling, award-winning US crime writer

'Richard Clark writes with great authority and a deep affection for his subject, which comes from his long association with Greece… Excellent.'

Marjory McGinn, author of *The Peloponnese Series, A Saint for the Summer* and *How Greek is Your Love?*

'*Return to Turtle Beach* is a heart-warming story that will transport you to the enchanting island of Crete.'

Maria A. Karamitsos, *My Greek Books*

'In *The Forgotten Song* the author weaves his magical prose to take the reader on a romantic journey with more twists and turns than a Cretan mountain pass.'

Tony Prouse, author and journalist

By the Same Author

The Greek Islands – A Notebook

Crete -- A Notebook

Rhodes – A Notebook

Corfu – A Notebook

Hidden Crete – A Notebook

More Hidden Crete – A Notebook

Eastern Crete – A Notebook

Richard Clark's Greek Islands Anthology

The Crete Trilogy

The Lost Lyra

Return to Turtle Beach

The Forgotten Song

The Crete Walking Society

First published in Great Britain and North America 2022

Copyright © Richard Clark 2022

Cover design © Mike Parsons 2022

All rights reserved. No part of this publication can be reproduced or transmitted in any form or by any means, electronic or mechanical, without permission in writing from Richard Clark.

Richard Clark has asserted his right to be identified as the author of this work in accordance with the Copyright, Designs and Patents Act, 1988.

ISBN – 9798405886053

www.facebook.com/richardclarkbooks

https://notesfromgreece.com

About the Author

Richard Clark is a writer, editor and journalist who has worked on an array of national newspapers and magazines in the UK. In 1982, on a whim, he decided to up sticks and live on the Greek island of Crete. So began a love affair that has continued to this day, and he still visits the Greek islands, where he has a home, on a regular basis. In 2016, he gave up the daily commute to London to become a full-time author. He is married with two grown up children and four grandchildren, and lives in Kent.

Acknowledgements

This book is a work of fiction, and although some real places have lent themselves as locations, many are the product of my imagination and all the characters are fictitious; any resemblance to real persons, living or dead, is purely coincidental. Any mistakes are mine.

A huge thank you goes to Tony and Bernadette Prouse for reading each chapter as it was produced and for their guidance. I am also grateful to the author Yvonne Payne for reading and giving her comments on the manuscript.

As always, I am lucky to be edited by the patient and meticulous Jennifer Barclay who has made this book better than it otherwise might have been. Again I am grateful to Mike Parsons for his beautiful cover design. Lastly, I must thank my family, Denise, Rebecca, James, Pete, Lucy, Esther, Imogen, Iris and Douglas for their unending support.

Note

The names of male Greek characters ending in an 's' will drop the letter in the vocative case (when that character is being addressed in direct speech).

For Bernadette and Tony

Prologue

2022

SOMEWHERE FAR BELOW the climbers could see lights twinkling, mirroring the stars that shone brightly above them in the clear night sky. Beyond the lights they could sense the invisible expanse of sea stretching away in the distance. Exhausted, Amy reached into her backpack and pulled out the sleeping bag. As the warmth of her elation at completing the climb wore off, she began to feel the chill of the night air grip her. She unrolled the bag and laid it down where the base of the wall of the tiny chapel of Timios

Stavros met the cold rock of the summit of Mount Ida. It would be daylight soon and she would be able to see what she had dreamed of for so long. Getting in, she felt herself cradled between church and mountain. She could hear the buzz of her friends talking, and made out the whispered tones of her sister Emma with Andrew, the affection in their voices like a lullaby. Amy smiled and drifted into sleep.

Staring into the darkness, Andrew sensed Emma shiver slightly. 'We made it,' said Emma.

'Look, the sun is coming up.' She took a step forward and stumbled on a small rock. Andrew grabbed her arm and stopped her from falling.

To the east, the bright fireball of the sun rose over the faraway Dhikti Mountains, signalling its intentions for a scorching day to come. To the west stood the White Mountains and below them to the south, as the cloud beneath them burned off, the coastal plain segued into the varnished waters of the Libyan Sea. The sight left the climbers spellbound; the silence only punctuated by the distant tinkling of goats' bells on the lower slopes.

As the group took in the panorama from the peak of Crete's tallest mountain, any tiredness, aches and pains they had felt after their night-time ascent were forgotten and they bathed in the early warmth of the sun and their achievement. From where they stood it was easy to forget the anxieties of the world below, struggling to heal itself from the pandemic which had transformed everybody's lives.

'Five more minutes and we must start our descent before the sun gets too hot.' The guide began to corral the climbers ready for the long walk down.

'Have you seen Amy?' Emma looked around for her older sister.

'She's over there.' Andrew pointed at the figure lying in the shadow of the crumbling stone walls of the tiny church.

Emma walked towards the chapel. 'I'll wake her up; she'll be upset if she misses this. It's a long way to come just for a snooze.'

Andrew laughed as Emma bent to rouse the sleeping Amy.

The Art of Survival

1992–2013

AMY PICKED UP a knife, mixed a hint of lemon yellow to the French ultramarine she had squirted onto her palette and dragged it across the canvas. Stepping back, she peered around the easel to get another look at the landscape. Seated nearby were the other members of the course, all working on delicate watercolours painted on pads on their laps.

The pebbled beach where Amy had placed her easel was in the shadow of the mountains which curved around the bay. Clusters of white houses dotted the olive-green lower slopes dropping down into the sea. Offshore, a small island floated in water of such intense bright blue that Amy was struggling to represent it on her canvas.

She felt the presence of Christos over her shoulder and took pride in the fact that his closeness sparked no feelings other than a desire for his encouragement. She turned and her course tutor smiled. He was undoubtedly handsome, so much so that he had been one of the reasons she had extended her trip to Crete. Giving in to his charm then, she had been flattered by his interest; he was so different from the few young students she had had brief relationships with at art college. But she had soon recognised his attentions and his painting were equally superficial.

'I can see you don't need me,' Christos said and grinned.

Amy held up a hand to stop her blonde hair blowing into her eyes and returned his smile.

'Thank you, Christo. I think I am fine at the moment. Perhaps one of the other ladies could do with your attention.' Amy gestured with her knife in the direction of the class members perched on portable stools on the beach.

'If I can help at all, just ask,' Christos said, striding towards a woman who was struggling as the paper on her pad fluttered in the breeze blowing in off the bay.

She laughed as he walked away. Amy did not regret her decision to stay on in Crete after her initial course and her affair with Christos had both ended. With the warmth of the sun on her back, staring out on this idyllic scene and doing what she most enjoyed, what was there to return to England for?

Amy had enjoyed her time at art school in London. There was no doubt it was a great place to study. When she was not painting at college, she would visit the galleries in search of inspiration or be talking long into the night with her fellow students.

After her graduation, reality struck; Britain was in a recession it couldn't shake off and finding any kind of employment, let alone as an artist, would have been difficult. The support she had had all the way through life from her parents was dwindling as they focussed on their separation, her father now only interested in his young girlfriend and her mother in protecting the emotional wellbeing of Amy's sister Emma, eleven years her junior.

Her mother had been angry when Amy phoned to tell her she was extending indefinitely what had originally been a month's visit to Crete. But here she could escape the grey depression of early nineties Britain and the disintegration of what had always been the security of her family.

In Crete the tourist industry was expanding rapidly, and Amy had no difficulty in finding a part-time job in a bar in Elounda. She found a room to rent in a village on the mountainside above the small resort and was content to spend her free time painting and enjoying the sunshine. The weeks turned into months and Amy fell into an easy routine. Most mornings she would swim in the warm waters of the bay. In the afternoons she would often join one of Christos' art classes, painting caiques in the harbour, or sometimes taking a minibus high up in the mountains to seek inspiration for their work.

She was developing her own style. Working in oils, she favoured the palette knife, making bold gestures on large canvasses as her paintings became progressively more abstract. Often they were too large to work on in the open air, and she took photographs or sketched her subject before returning to her small, bright apartment to paint.

Her relationship with Christos was relaxed. Both of them knew where they stood. When she had first arrived on the island she had been open to a fling with her art teacher, but was not naïve enough to think there was any long-term future with him. Now she laughed as she witnessed him practice the same charms she had fallen for on any number of his pupils. In turn, Christos loved having Amy join his groups, taking proprietorial pride in her prodigious talent, although they both knew that this was something she had arrived with and had little to do with his mentoring.

Joining the group also allowed her to showcase her work to the amateur watercolourists who came on Christos' painting holidays. Selling a few pieces helped her afford her modest lifestyle. Her talents did not go unnoticed among the locals either and, as time went on, several shops in Elounda and further afield exhibited and sold her paintings.

Within a few years of arriving on the island, Amy saved enough money that, when added to a small inheritance when her godfather died, she was able to buy an old house in Epano Elounda. The two-bedroom traditional cottage was run down but sound. Amy had been patient in its restoration, teaching herself to do most of the work, taking pleasure in slowly bringing the house back to life. Inside and out she had scrubbed the walls before scraping off any flaking paint, then sanding and recoating with new whitewash. She had stripped the window frames, shutters and doors to bare wood before filling, sanding and painting in several new coats of blue gloss.

Over time she managed to furnish it simply with bits and pieces kindly given by neighbours or bought second-hand or occasionally new with her wages or the sale of a painting. Upstairs in the house was a bedroom and an airy room opening out onto a terrace which she turned into a studio. On cooler days or if the sun was too hot she would paint inside but, if she could, she loved to paint in the open air on the terrace. The view from here was what Amy loved most about the house. During the day she could see waves of silver olive trees stretching to the Bay of Korfos. At night she could look up at the stars in the clearest of skies and down at Elounda as the solitary lights from small fishing boats tracked their course towards the canal that connected the bay to the open waters of Mirabello.

An old donkey track led from the village to Elounda and the bay. Every morning Amy would delight in the twenty-minute walk through the olive groves to drink a coffee in one of the waterfront tavernas and buy her daily bread before returning home.

Her house was on the edge of the village and sat in a tiny olive grove. If the cottage had been dilapidated when she first bought it, the olive trees had been cared for by neighbours and, with their help and advice, Amy learned to take care of her few trees. In the late autumn she would lay out nets on the ground and friends from the village would help her take on the backbreaking work of beating the olives from the trees. She would provide a picnic for the families who came to help, the children sorting the leaves and stalks from the crop before the olives were loaded into hessian sacks. She took pride in the small amount of oil they yielded when she delivered her harvest to be pressed.

To the front of the house was a small garden which Amy had cleared and planted with geraniums, red, pink and white. She loved the time she spent in the early mornings watering the flowers, picking the ripe fruit from the lemon and fig trees that grew there or watching the progress of the lilac-coloured bougainvillea which was slowly covering the whitewashed walls of the cottage.

Her property was flanked by a larger olive grove on one side and a small house on the other, barely visible through the overgrown garden which year by year was encroaching on the tumbledown structure. Amy loved the way that the earth appeared to be reclaiming the neglected building, but she had not dared to go closer, scared of what might be slithering in the undergrowth.

When the weeds began to climb over the grey stone wall which marked the boundaries between her garden and her neighbour's, she would cut them back so they didn't overrun her own garden and olive grove. But there was something about the wildness of the next-door plot that she found fascinating. She painted the house from her terrace, the stripped bare wood of its front door hanging off rusted hinges, hiding behind the tendrils of climbing weeds. Over the years she made a series of paintings and drawings, a record of how nature was returning the land to its own.

Strangely, Amy did not feel the pull of her homeland. The village and Elounda catered for most of her day-to-day needs, and sometimes she would catch a bus to the nearby town of Agios Nikolaos to buy art supplies. After doing her shop she would stop for a coffee in one of the many tavernas that surrounded the picturesque lake in the town. Soon the waiters and taverna owners came to know the smiling English artist who made every effort to greet them and make her order in a halting Greek, which over the years blossomed into a fluency that was impressive for a foreigner.

If she had few regrets about leaving England, she did miss her little sister Emma who wrote regularly, her letters at first documenting the breakup of their parents' marriage through a child's eyes, then her difficult years as a teenager growing up. Amy returned to England every few years. She could tell that her sister was well loved, even spoiled by her mother, for whom Emma was her only close family.

While her young sibling was held close in her mother's protective embrace and showered with love, Amy saw that even when she did return home, her mother found it difficult to hide the resentment she felt towards the daughter who she considered had abandoned her. It was when Amy returned to Crete that she felt at home. As the aeroplane cabin doors opened at Heraklion airport, bringing the smell of wild herbs from the mountains and salt from the sea, she experienced a feeling of wellbeing which somehow eluded her in England.

Six years after her arrival on Crete, Christos announced that he was getting married to a girl from Kritsa, a village in the mountains to the southwest of Agios Nikolaos. His future father-in-law had offered him a job running a taverna he owned and the newly married couple would live in an apartment above the business. Christos would stop running his art workshops. Amy smiled at the news, and could understand why his fiancée's jealousy and her family's concern would see them keen to put a stop to his art classes, and any activities associated with them.

Amy had continued with the art workshops out of habit and when they stopped she found the extra time she had to pursue her own painting projects liberating. By now her artwork was established and selling well. Over the many years she lived on the island she had had several exhibitions in Elounda, Agios Nikolaos and even in Heraklion. It was at her first exhibition in the island's capital that she had met Nick. She was attracted to the tall, tanned man, quite a few years older than her, as he stood pondering one of her paintings. She had plucked up the courage to approach him and ask him what he thought of the picture and introduced herself as the artist.

She was flattered that he understood and liked her work, and he was impressed with her talent as well as her casual beauty and open smile. They never really agreed to go out, but that first encounter had led to a drink which turned into a meal which developed into a friendship. Nick was an archaeologist who taught at a university in the UK. He spent his summers in Crete taking students on various digs, about which he was passionate. Amy loved his enthusiasm for ancient history and was attracted to the bronzed, angular body, rugged features and self-deprecating smile of the academic. He in turn found her a kindred spirit in her passion for the island and loved the way she could express her innermost feeling for it through her paintings.

The two of them fell into an easy relationship, each demanding little, making the days they had together more special. Both seemed to flourish with the freedoms their affair allowed them. Outside the time they spent together they were happy to make no demands of each other. Amy was at ease in her own company, but delighted to seize the chance of happiness shared with another person should it present itself. Still, she was wary of commitment following the dissolution of her parents' relationship and cherished the liberty she had forged in her life on the island.

Amy absorbed herself in painting and sketching, and the sales of her artwork had allowed her to give up her waitressing job in the bar. If money got tight she would paint small watercolours for the tourist market or decorate ceramics for a potter she knew in a neighbouring village. Although she maintained a comfortable income, for the most part she lived a frugal lifestyle. When not working she would walk in the mountains above the village or travel further afield to climb through some of the island's dramatic gorges.

Many a night she would spend in the local taverna. Amy loved the stark simplicity and cheerful informality of this centre of village social life. The owner, Alexander, had taken to the foreigner living in the village and over the years Amy had become part of his family. He was proud to have such a talented artist as a friend and was not shy in telling his customers about her work.

When Amy first moved to the village, she had been the only outsider living there. But as the years passed, others had discovered the delights of its seclusion. With some houses becoming empty as locals moved to the coast to work in tourism, one by one they were bought by people from abroad, who eventually became a small group of outsiders living in the village.

What came to be known as the 'walking society' was not really a society at all in any formal sense, but a group of people who shared an interest in walking. It had begun when Amy returned from one of her regular treks and had got talking to Juliette, a newcomer to the village from France whom Alexander had introduced her to. The two women had made friends easily and, by the time Amy planned her next trip, it seemed only natural to invite Juliette along. Over the months and years that followed, others both Greek and foreign joined them, and it became customary for them to gather once a month for a hike together.

For the members, the society was so much more than just a club for people with a shared interest in walking. It became a support network; for newcomers, it helped them to establish themselves in their adopted country. Friendships were made and sometimes closer relationships were forged and the meetings of the group became as important as the regular expeditions.

Most Fridays, Alexander would push together tables, wedging beer mats under them on the uneven flagstone floor, before serving mezzes washed down with jugs of wine. Sometimes he would break from the kitchen and take a lyra from where it hung on the wall and play. Inhibitions loosened by the wine, and roused by the soaring melody of the lyra, the friends would get up and dance alongside the locals in the taverna.

Over the year, Nick visited the island as often as he could. As well as the long summer break, he would fly out at Christmas and Easter and during term-time 'reading weeks' and, if his teaching commitments allowed, he would join the group both in the taverna on a Friday night and on their hikes. Amy enjoyed his company and was pleased when he was there. The rest of the group appreciated his presence, not just because of his friendly and knowledgeable companionship, but because he had the use of a minibus in which he transported his students on weekdays and at weekends he could drive his friends to treks further afield.

On one such night in the taverna Nick learned to his amazement that, despite having lived on the island for nearly twenty-one years, Amy had not walked the Samaria Gorge. And she was not alone amongst the group. It was something Amy had always meant to do, but for one reason or another she had not got around to making the journey west to take on the hike down the longest gorge in Europe. Uplifted by a cocktail of Nick's descriptions of the ravine and the wine itself, they all readily agreed to his suggestion that they should tackle the walk together. Orthodox Easter fell in May that year, in a fortnight's time, and coincided with Amy's forty-second birthday. It was decided the trek would be a wonderful way to mark the occasion.

A plan was put into place. Nick would drive them to the small seaside town of Paleochora on the south-west coast. They would stay overnight before making an early start to reach the mouth of the gorge the next morning. They could leave the minibus at the top. After completing the ten-mile trek to the bottom of the canyon, they would catch a ferry to the seaside village of Sougia where they would stay overnight, then the following morning Nick would take a taxi to the head of the gorge to collect the minibus before driving back to Sougia to pick up his friends.

Eight others decided to join Nick and Amy for the long weekend away. The couple agreed to meet Juliette and her boyfriend Mike first outside the church of Zoodoho Pigi in Epano Elounda. They would then drive to the quayside in Elounda and pick up Emer, a retired Irish teacher of English and her Greek husband Georgios; Stelios, a young doctor, and his fiancée Suzi, a lawyer; Petra, a Dutch woman who was a part-time instructor at the local diving school; and Rob, who had arrived on the island as crew on a yacht and just stayed.

*

The Easter weekend came, and the group chatted excitedly that morning as Nick pulled away from the waterfront onto the road passing tavernas and shops, avoiding double parked cars and early morning tour coaches coming in the opposite direction. They hooted and waved at friends from the village going about their business before the bus began the climb up the mountainside. Although they all knew the road well, they instinctively turned to see the Bay of Korfos below; its stunning beauty never disappointed despite its familiarity. In the distance they could see the island of Spinalonga guarding the northern reaches of the bay which flowed through the narrow canal beneath them into Mirabello, a bridge from the causeway joining it with the island of Kalydon. Somewhere submerged by the mirror-like waters was the lost city of Olous. As they reached Lenika, they could see the Bay of Mirabello and the mountains to the east above the glittering town of Agios Nikolaos.

By the time the minibus was straining up the long climb to the monastery at Selinari, Amy turned to see that several of her companions had succumbed to the heat and early start and were dozing while those awake stared at the mesmerising view.

'Look there!' Nick said, at the same time swinging the bus into the pull-off outside the monastery. He jumped out and slid open the side doors, pointing up to the sky. Flying over the mountain, a pair of griffon vultures rode the thermals, their giant wings holding them majestically as they scanned the mountainside for food.

'I thought we weren't stopping, except for food or fuel,' laughed Amy. She knew that Nick was unable to pass the monastery of St George at Selinari; although he would not admit it, he was unwilling to risk the bad luck many Greeks believed would befall those who failed to break their journey there. Secretly Georgios, Stelios and Suzi were pleased he had, and somehow seeing the vultures had uplifted the languid mood. When they got on their way again the friends were all chatting as they sped along the national road that cut through the mountains, bypassing the popular coastal resorts of Malia and Hersonissos before reaching the island capital of Heraklion.

Heading west of the city, they began to climb again as the road weaved its way among the olive groves which covered the hillsides. Through a forest of pine, the road was lined with stalls selling oranges hanging in blue and yellow plastic bags from the roofs of makeshift huts. To the south, in the distance, they could see the foothills of Psiloritis, Crete's tallest mountain.

A little over two hours into the journey Nick could see the disappointment on Amy's face.

'We can stop if you'd like.' He knew that she loved the medieval splendour of Rethymnon and the bustling narrow streets of its old town which radiated out from the Venetian harbour.

'No, we need to keep going. But thanks for thinking of me.' Amy patted Nick's leg as he drove past the exit to the town. She knew they still had some way to go, and that it would be unfair on Nick if he didn't have time to relax in Paleochora after his long drive. In another hour they had made it to Chania; again they didn't stop but drove past the city and on to Maleme where they turned south on a road that switchbacked over the hinterland of the White Mountains.

Everyone was now wide awake as Nick coaxed the bus around the sharp bends and up and down the steep inclines. All around them, the ground rose up or fell steeply away. In the distance, on the higher peaks they could see snow, beneath which the bare limestone outlined the slopes against the clear blue Cretan sky. This was the wildest and least visited area of Crete. In her twenty-one years on the island, Amy had never travelled to these parts. She marvelled at how anyone could make a living from this seemingly barren land, though olive, fig and walnut trees clung to the slopes and sheep and goats nibbled at the scrubby ground. As they passed through villages, elderly men wearing the traditional Cretan dress, their trousers tucked into long boots, looked up from the taverna tables where they sat.

Descending southwards they could see the Libyan Sea before suddenly the road flattened out as it felt its way towards a peninsula in the shadow of the mountains. They drove down an avenue of eucalyptus trees through a plain covered with olive groves and polytunnels filled with tomatoes growing on the vines, before the road trickled into the small town of Paleochora.

The following morning it was still dark when the friends got into the minibus. Amy accepted murmured wishes of happy birthday as they climbed aboard. Nick stopped outside the bakery and they bought warm cheese and spinach pies and coffees for breakfast, and filled baguettes to put in their packs. The aroma of the newly baked pastry and coffee flooded the van and they were tucking in as Nick drove into the foothills of the mountains. As they climbed higher so did their spirits. Sitting in the front passenger seat, Amy broke off pieces of pie to feed to Nick on the short straights between the hairpin bends as the road threaded through the mountains.

The sun began to rise and slowly revealed the landscape. For some, being able to see the precipitous drops to the side of the road was a mixed blessing. The roadside shrines bore testament to the precarious nature of the route but as daylight began to fill in the colours of the trees and rocks it was impossible not to be awestruck.

Their early start had paid off and the group was pleased to see they were the first walkers of the day to begin the trek. Paying their entrance fee, they set off along a path which turned into steps dropping steeply down into a valley densely forested with pines and cypresses. Their morale was good at the prospect of the descent from the Omalos Plateau to the sea some 1200 metres below.

While they walked, Nick explained how the gorge had been carved out of the limestone and granite by a river. Over thousands of years the erosion had created this wonder of nature in the shadow of the White Mountains. He told them that the mountain range was so named because its colour never changed: in the winter the peaks were shrouded in snow and in the warmer weather they glowed white as the sunshine reflected off the limestone. The range of mountains they were descending from was enormous, the largest on the island, covering 300 square miles of the remote southwest. The tallest peak was that of Mount Pachnes, at 2453 metres just three metres shorter than Mount Ida in the Psiloritis range to the east, the highest on Crete. Amy was amused to hear that, at the apex of Pachnes, some proud locals had piled rocks in an attempt to make it stand taller than its rival.

With the sun still low in the sky there was a chill in the air as they delved deeper down into the valley. Smells of wild marjoram, eucalyptus and pine infused the atmosphere as they criss-crossed the gurgling stream that ran through the gorge. Was it possible that this benign trickle was partly responsible for creating such an imposing formation? Nick told them that in the winter the stream swelled to a raging torrent fed by rain and meltwaters from the mountains. During those months the park was closed to visitors as hiking there was too dangerous.

Gradually the walking group spread out, some pausing to take photographs whilst others slowed to take in the beauty around them. Amy could not have imagined a more memorable way to celebrate her birthday. Moments like this were a confirmation that it had been the right decision to make her life in Crete. Strolling through this wonder of nature, she felt more at ease than she could have imagined when she had left her home in England to join a painting course more than twenty-one years ago.

She slowed to watch Nick, letting him walk ahead, his thin, angular frame agile as he traversed the rocks and boulders. He stopped and turned, raising a hand to brush away a strand of long greying hair which had fallen across his face. She smiled at the thought of how uncomplicated their relationship was, how unlike that of her parents whose marriage had ended in divorce around the time she had escaped to Crete. She loved Nick's enthusiasm for the world around him and his thirst for knowledge; it matched the passion she had for painting, both in their own way expressing their joy at being alive.

Standing on a boulder, Nick raised a finger to his lips, signalling for her to be quiet as he pointed with the other hand to a clearing in the trees. Amy followed his finger just in time to see what looked like a goat run for the cover of the forest.

'Did you see the kri-kri?' Nick whispered.

Amy had seen a number of tavernas on the island with that name but had never seen the animal in the flesh. She stared in the direction it had run, but there was no sign of it.

'I didn't get much of a look,' replied Amy. 'It's a goat?'

'Similar, officially it's an indigenous ibex that is unique to the island. They're part of the reason that the gorge was established as a national park – as a reserve to protect them.' Nick handed her his water bottle. 'They're important to Cretans as they're a living link to their past. They feature clearly on Minoan frescoes and in jewellery from that period too. Their long, curved horns are so distinctive they could hardly be anything else.'

'Why do they need protecting?' asked Amy.

'Things are getting better now, thanks to strict conservation laws and reserves like this. During the German occupation of the island in the Second World War, the people were starving and hunted the kri-kri for food. After the war it was estimated there were fewer than two hundred surviving. I think those numbers have now risen into the thousands.'

On the other side of the clearing Amy noticed a small church and was drawn towards it. She took some respite from the sun in the shade of the stone walls. Looking around she could see the tumbledown remains of several buildings and one that had been restored as a warden's office.

'This is the chapel of Osia Maria, or Saint Mary – from which the village of Samaria got its name,' said Nick as he sat down beside her. 'There was a village here?' asked Amy, surprised.

'Since Byzantine times. The last villagers left their homes here in 1962 to accommodate the park.'

Sitting in silence, Amy painted a picture in her mind, restoring the ramshackle stones which lay around the clearing to how they might have been half a century before. She breathed in the splendour of the mountains that surrounded her and the beauty of the wildflowers which grew anywhere they could take hold. She tried to imagine what life must have been like for those who had lived here. Today the rugged terrain looked benign, but the isolation must have been onerous and the living precarious. In winter the turbulent waters and snows would have cut off the community. She wondered if any of the villagers were still alive and if they regretted being relocated.

A few others had now caught up with them, and sat down on boulders strewn around the valley floor to rest and have a drink. Amy wandered alone for a moment, thinking about how her move away from the place in which she had grown up had changed her. There was little that she would want to be any different about her life now. She was happy in her own skin and self-contained. She loved having the time to paint. Her relationship with Nick provided well for her emotional needs and looking around at her companions from the walking society, she valued and enjoyed their friendship but did not rely on their company.

Amy returned to the others and smiled as she listened to Nick now explaining to Juliette and Mike how the isolation of the gorge had made it an ideal hiding place for resistance fighters during the war. The invading army was reluctant to enter the narrow ravine as its steep-sided walls made it easy to defend. She laughed inside at the way her boyfriend couldn't resist the teacher in him coming out; but his enthusiasm to share his knowledge was infectious and she felt a warm sense of pride as she watched her friends hang on his words.

When they resumed their walk downhill towards the coast, the gorge narrowed and the sheer vertical rock faces closed in on either side of them, reaching upwards and obliterating the sun. Looking up, the sky appeared a distant rip in the cloak of rock. They were approaching the narrowest part of the gorge. One by one the friends stretched out their arms trying to touch both sides of the ravine but each fell short by some two metres. Craning their necks again here, the rock towered above them at least 300 metres. For a moment the group stood in awe, silent in the face of such majesty, tiny dots at the bottom of this monumental natural wonder.

From here the going got easier, but the walkers had to be careful not to trip on the boulders which littered their path as they followed the course of the river along its final few miles to the Libyan Sea. A goatherd in traditional Sfakiot dress stopped to watch, his head resting on his crook, as they picked their way across the rocks. He nodded as Amy wished him *kalimera*.

Ending the walk at the beach of the village of Agia Roumeli, after the shade of the gorge the sun was hot. The walkers stopped for a cold beer at a taverna before heading for a swim. It was still early in the year and the sea was cold enough to take their breath away. Adjusting to the cool temperature, Amy floated on her back, looking up at the clear blue sky. Buoyed up in the salty water, she warmed her body under the gaze of the hot sun, soothing any aches she had from the trek and as she floated, she could not think of a better way she could have spent her birthday. She rolled onto her front and looked down through the clear water to the rocks below. An octopus scuttled across the sea bed. Raising her head, she heard shrieks as Rob swum up to Petra, pulling her under by the legs. Stelios and Suzi stood knee deep in water near the shore talking while the others sat on the beach.

Amy could feel herself burning and taking long, languid strokes she swam to the shore, making her unsteady way across the pebbles to where the others sat. The ferry to take them along the coast to Sougia was not due for several hours so they returned to the taverna for a leisurely lunch, sharing plates of souvlaki, goat, pork chops and rabbit alongside a horta omelette made with wild greens picked from the mountainside, and salads. The food tasted wonderful after the exertions of the hike and the group cleared every dish that had been placed in front of them.

The friends then sat in comfortable indolence, nibbling on watermelon and grapes while they waited to spot their ship appearing around the headland. At first a dot on the horizon, the small car ferry *Samaria* came into focus, the snub nose of the raised ramp pushing aside a white wave across an otherwise flawless blue sea. By the time they had paid the bill, gathered up their backpacks and made their way to the short quay on the waterfront, the vessel was being edged bow first towards its berth.

Not to waste time since no vehicles were disembarking, the skipper navigated close to the quay and dispensed with the need to moor, the engines keeping it on station as the ramp was dropped with a clang. Barely were the last of the passengers aboard before the ship went astern, pulling away from the shore while the ramp was still being raised. As the group made their way upstairs to the top deck, the ship thrust forwards in a gentle arc towards the west. Finding a seat on the starboard side by the rail, Amy and Nick squeezed in beside the backpacks, poles and other paraphernalia of their fellow passengers. Looking up, Amy could see the misty outline of the moon already sharing the evening sky with a sun descending towards the headlands ahead.

It seemed like no time before they were coasting alongside a long strip of deserted beach which lined a long, sweeping bay, stippled with occasional clusters of umbrellas and sun loungers.

They could just make out a row of tavernas beside the beach and the ferry changed course for a quay on the outer wall of a small harbour to the west of the village. Sougia was a sleepy, rundown place, offering little but tavernas and rooms to rent and a few shops. For the friends it was none the worse for that. They had already booked for their overnight stay. In their room, Amy showered and changed whilst Nick went to see the taxi company to confirm arrangements for the following day.

Darkness had fallen by the time the friends started out to choose a restaurant in which to celebrate Amy's birthday. Tired but elated after the day's successful trek, they walked along the coast road stopping at each taverna, debating the merits of their menu. They were spoiled for choice; although it was Easter, the locals would not break their fast until the following day. They picked a taverna looking out over the bay, its tables under a pergola garlanded with vines. Tubs on the terrace were resplendent with early blooming geraniums.

As Amy stared out to sea, she could hear the silence, feeling its soothing powers grounding her as the buzz of chatter subsided into the background. A wash from some ship far out to sea ruffled the stillness as it whispered its way up the beach.

'Is that OK with you, Amy?' Interrupted from her reverie, she turned to Nick. 'Sorry, I was miles away.'

'We just wondered if we should order a mixture and all share. It's so difficult to choose. What do you think?' said Nick.

'That's great with me. I was struggling to make my mind up anyway. What a perfect spot,' Amy continued. 'I'm pleased you brought us here.' Nick smiled and took her hand, letting it drop again as the waiter came to take their order. First jugs of local wine, both red and white, were brought and then the food began to arrive. Rooster in a red wine sauce, deep fried courgette flowers stuffed with feta cheese and herbs, goat cooked with wild almonds, rabbit and creamy mizithra cheese, deep purple beetroot and bitter horta harvested from the mountains.

In the distance they could make out the sound of a lyra being played somewhere along the coast as though it had sprung fresh from the mountains which towered around them. Few people were out and about, the locals no doubt staying at home preparing for the late-night church service and the end of their fast. Along the road a charcoal grill was being erected in preparation for the following day's Easter feast and a solitary old woman dressed all in black bustled purposefully towards the church of Agios Panteleimon.

Amy loved the Easter celebrations on Crete. Something in the permanence of the traditions which had remained unchanged for centuries made her feel secure. Looking out to sea, a wave of blissful tiredness washed over her.

The sound of Nick tapping a fork against his wine glass interrupted her thoughts. He rose to his feet as the friends hushed. 'I hope you don't mind, but I just wanted to say a few words. First of all, Happy Birthday to Amy, and thank you to her for organising this trip.' The friends raised their glasses and echoed Nick's wishes. Amy laughed, colouring slightly at the attention. Nick remained standing, and continued speaking. 'I have another announcement I would like to make. I have been offered a job, a professorship in America starting in September.' As Amy froze, she heard a ripple of congratulations amongst her friends, before feeling their eyes settle on her. What was Nick doing pushing his chair away from the table and getting down on one knee. 'Will you marry me Amy and come with me to America?'

Amy's mind went into slow motion. In that instant her world had shifted from contentment and been pitched into uncertainty. Through her misted vision she could see him fumble in his pocket and pull out a small box and open the lid. What was Nick thinking? A few minutes earlier she could not have been happier; now she was in turmoil. Amy stood, pushing back her chair with her legs and, without being aware of what she was doing, ran. Stopping to catch her breath she looked back and saw Nick still on his knees and her friends struck silent watching her hurried departure.

Tears streamed down her face as she found the cover of darkness and slowed to a fast walk along the street in the direction of the small harbour. As the tears flowed, she walked past tavernas, some empty and dimly lit, others closed. Along the dark street she could make out the shadowy figures of people making their way towards the church. She sniffed and wiped a sleeve across her eyes to hide her embarrassment. But in the gloom nobody could see the torment that she felt.

She found herself at the quay and made her way round to the rocks where they dropped into the sea near the narrow harbour entrance. In the moonlight she could make out the colours of the small boats serenely swaying on their moorings: a few fishing boats and caiques, a water taxi and small open pleasure launches. Beyond, the sea was silent but she could sense its depth beneath the surface. In the distance she could make out the almost imperceptible line where it met a sky flecked with stars, shining their bright messages from a past thousands of years ago somewhere in the galaxy.

Now she found it impossible to focus, her mind racing between what had just happened and a future she had not expected or desired. She loved Nick in her own way, but didn't he understand that part of that love was the freedom their relationship offered them both? Her stability was rooted in this island which she had chosen to make her home, in which so much of her happiness was invested. Slowing her breathing, she peered into the darkness.

Amy was certain of one thing as she tried to piece her thoughts back together, she owed it to Nick to talk and explain how she felt. She did not understand how after all these years he could have made such a devastating misjudgement. But she was sure it had been made through love and, whatever the gulf it had revealed between their expectations, she knew that Nick would be hurting.

How long she had been there staring out to sea she did not know. The calm of the ocean had steadied her thoughts and she knew the answer she had to give to Nick. She stood up from the rock and made her way back to the road towards the village. Outside the church of Agios Panteleimon she stopped. A couple of men stood smoking by the door. The building was unexceptional, white stone roofed with terracotta tiles; a covered terrace ran along one side and a bell tower stood apart in the graveyard which surrounded it. Amy stopped and looked at the church, so striking in its simplicity. From inside she could hear the chanting of the priest and the murmurings of the congregation. The two men threw down their cigarette butts and opened the doors, and slipped back inside.

Amy looked at her watch. It was nearly midnight. She knew that the villagers would be preparing for the most sacred moment of the year when they celebrated the resurrection of Christ. Candles would be lit from the Holy Light passed amongst them by the priest, gradually giving light to the darkness.

The door of the church opened as the hour struck midnight. Amy could hear the priest chanting *'Christos anesti,'* Christ is risen, as he led the congregation outside. She started as a young man toting a gun fired a salvo of shots in the air, the cue for children and their fathers to throw firecrackers, and somewhere in the distance a firework illuminated the night sky. Turning, she continued towards the village, dreading the conversation that must be had but knowing it could not be avoided.

As she neared the taverna, she could hear her friends talking about what had happened. There was no sign of Nick. Through the darkness she could make out Suzi's concerned voice calling her. She raised a hand in an unsure gesture, and slipped back into the shadows. Casting her eyes seawards she spotted the silhouette of a solitary figure on the beach.

Nick sat looking out to sea; he was desperately seeking something his thoughts could cling to. How had he misread his relationship with Amy so badly? Had he been so flattered by the offer of a job which fulfilled his lifetime's ambition that it had blinded him to the reality of their bond? A cool breeze tickled the sea where it met the shore and Nick shivered as he listened to the water's sigh. Shutting himself off from all but the whispers around him he glanced in his mind's eye the truth he had not seen in his haste to plan out his future with Amy. He realised that this island, more than anything, was fundamental to her being. To take her away from it would be like stealing something from her soul. Crete to Amy was like academic ambition was to him, and he had been so bound up in that dream that he had not recognised what was elemental to the woman he loved.

Steps on the pebbles alerted him. He turned to see Amy. As he stood, she put her arms around him and in that hug they both knew that it was over. Both loved the other enough to let each of them hold on to their dreams.

'I'm sorry,' Nick whispered. 'I'm sorry too.' Amy took his hand and led him up the beach then let it drop. As they made their way back to the room, they heard the sporadic bangs of firecrackers and, along the road, huddles of people protected the flames of candles and chatted excitedly at the prospect of the Easter celebrations.

Although melancholy, Amy found herself smiling as they passed families so caught up in these timeless rituals. She considered how this weekend might be the last time she spent with

Nick. It surprised her that, although the thought saddened her, she was not as overwrought as she had been at the prospect of leaving Crete and getting married. In the end, few words had been needed to bring their relationship to a close.

Back in their room, Nick sat reading, leaving the bed for Amy. When she awoke, memories of the night before filtered into her head. Beside her on the pillow lay a note. Nick had already left to get a taxi to the head of Samaria Gorge and pick up the minibus. She opened the shutters. Out to sea, a lone ship made its way towards the horizon, heading for Africa.

Island of Dreams

2016-2020

ISABELLE AND ANDREW had first visited Crete when they took a break from their work on Lesvos. They had met in the Moria refugee camp, where Isabelle was a doctor and Andrew was reporting on the refugee crisis for his newspaper in London. Amidst the despair of so many displaced souls who had made it across the straits to Europe from Turkey, somehow the couple had found love. As Isabelle fought day and night to care for the health needs of the ever-increasing numbers who had made the crossing,

Andrew worked ceaselessly to meet his incessant news deadlines and tell the story of the victims of war, famine and political upheaval who had risked their all to find a better life.

For Andrew the attraction had been instant. As soon as he had seen Isabelle, he had been drawn to the tall, slim, blonde-haired woman whose calm, confident compassion appeared to give reassurance to the distressed souls she had to relentlessly deal with. She in turn found the lean, dark-haired journalist attractive, and as she got to know him found in his company a place she could open up and shed the tensions of her day-to-day life.

In the moments when they weren't working or sleeping, the couple sought solace in each other. Over time this had developed into a relationship which helped them deal with the horror and suffering that occupied most of their waking hours. Finding time together was difficult with the demands of their jobs and in late spring, when they managed to contrive a fortnight's leave that coincided, they decided to escape, island-hopping by ferry to Chios, Mykonos and on to Crete.

Most of the journey they spent on deck talking, looking over the rail for islands on the horizon or snoozing in each other's arms as the ferries transported them southwards. As they left Lesvos further and further behind, with every mile they sailed it felt as though a weight was being lifted from their shoulders. Both of them loved their work, but it was only when they got away from the island that they comprehended the pressures their jobs had put them under, confronting the constant human pain.

Poring over a guidebook, they excitedly made plans. There was so much they wanted to see but Crete was large and they didn't want to spend much of their available time travelling. They decided that since the ferry docked in the island's capital, they would visit the Minoan palace of Knossos a few miles south of the city as soon as they arrived. Given her work as a doctor to people who had been forced to leave behind their homes, Isabelle was also particularly fascinated by the story of the former leper island of Spinalonga in the east, and the surrounding villages looked like they would be perfect places to search for a pension for their short stay.

As the ship came into dock, they stood on deck staring in wonder at the striking Venetian fortress at the mouth of the adjacent old harbour, which was full of fishing boats, caiques and a myriad of pleasure craft. Disembarking, they squeezed their way through the crowd of people waiting to welcome friends and relatives or hawking their rooms to rent. Making their way past the imposing walls of the vaulted Venetian arsenals, they headed uphill towards the centre of the city along the bustling 25 August Street.

Avoiding the attentions of waiters' eager to secure their custom, they found a car rental shop and hired a vehicle for the duration of their stay. Isabelle took the wheel with Andrew reading the map. They followed the coast road before cutting inland, bypassing the city and finally turning off for Knossos.

After queuing for some time, they gained entrance to the Minoan palace. The heat and the crowds somehow diminished the enjoyment of the experience, although there was no doubt that the site was extraordinary. Seeing past the tour groups and blotting out the sound of hundreds of clicking camera shutters, the couple imagined what life had been like for the people who had lived there nearly 4,000 years ago. Reading in the guidebook about how the site was enthusiastically restored by the aristocratic English archaeologist Sir Arthur Evans, they were unsure how they felt about the reconstruction of the palace and its surroundings, but it was hard not to be drawn to the vibrant three red pillars framing a fresco of a bull.

Turning their backs on the painting, the expanse of the whole palace was laid out in front of them: more than a thousand interconnecting rooms surrounding a square which had been the centre of what Evans named the Minoan civilisation after the mythical King Minos of Crete. A jumble of myths and historical facts had been entwined into the legend of the labyrinth, the deadly lair of the Minotaur, dug beneath the palace by the master builder Daedalus. In such surroundings, it was impossible to resist being enchanted.

That first day on Crete, Isabelle and Andrew both realised they had fallen in love, not only with each other but with the magical island itself. As they drove east away from Knossos the landscape became more stunning and put them under its spell.

Andrew drove back to the main highway heading eastwards. As he drove the landscape became more rugged. Rising up, the road cut between two mountains. Boulders were strewn on the edges of the road, evidence of some recent landfall. As they climbed they could see a four-tiered bell tower, which their guidebook told them was the monastery of Agios Georgios, Selinari, rising through the forested slopes.

Leaving the monastery behind, they drove through a land fertile with olive trees, orange groves, and orchards of almonds. The hillsides were sprinkled with villages of whitewashed houses and the skeletons of tumbledown stone windmills stood by the roadside. The open car windows provided little relief from the scorching sun, but the smells of mountain herbs which blew in on the breeze laced the air with promise.

In the heat, Isabelle struggled to stay awake but was determined not to succumb to sleep. On the outskirts of the town of Agios

Nikolaos, Andrew turned the car off the main road, following a sign to Elounda. As the road cut back on itself, heading north, the cliffs dropped away into the deep blue of the Aegean Sea. Turning around, Isabelle could make out the glimmering town behind them as they climbed higher and higher.

If she was struggling with keeping her eyes open before they reached the top, the view which met the couple as they reached Lenika put all thoughts of sleep out of her head. Far below them they could make out a narrow canal that linked two bays. In the distance the island of Spinalonga sparkled like a diamond set in a sapphire sea. Isabelle thought she had never seen anything like it in all her life. Something about it soothed her soul and she knew she had found her spiritual home. She turned to look at Andrew who was finding it difficult keeping his eyes on the road. This was the beginning of their long-term dream to make a life for themselves on the island.

Wakes from boats crossing the bay wove filigree patterns on the calm waters as they descended into Elounda. As the road flattened out it narrowed to thread its way through a cluster of shops and apartments before opening out onto a bustling square. The *plateia* apparently acted as a car park for the village, flanked on one side by tavernas and on the other by a quay bobbing with brightly painted caiques.

'It's splendid! I'm starving – shall we stop and get something to eat here?' Isabelle asked as Andrew spotted someone vacating a parking space and swung the hire car into it.

'Sounds like a plan.' It was getting late in the afternoon and the village looked busy, and Andrew was anxious they might not find somewhere to stay.

Isabelle was keen to sit right beside the bay and they found a taverna on the road which ran aong the seafront.

'Sit where you like.' The friendly waiter held out an arm, gesturing to the tables under the shade by the water's edge.

They chose a table beside which the gin-clear water almost lapped at their feet. Looking down they could make out the shimmer of silver fish swimming and both sat back in the cushioned chairs and inhaled the warm sea air. Just offshore a blue-and-white caique lay at anchor. In the distance a large island was connected to the mainland by the bridge over the canal which they had spotted from the mountain top.

'Look, I think that's Spinalonga.' Andrew pointed and Isabelle turned her head to see the small island floating at the northern entrance to the bay.

'Yes, that's Spinalonga.' They had not heard the waiter approach, so entranced were they by the delightful setting. 'Would you like a drink perhaps?'

'I'd love a beer,' said Isabelle. 'I'll have one too,' said Andrew. 'Do you mind if I just go and see if I can find us a room?'

'How long you staying for? Maybe I can help,' replied the waiter. 'My aunt has an apartment above her home. She rents it out. It is not so far. It is in a small village in the mountains, maybe two kilometres from here. If you like I phone her and ask if it is free.'

Andrew saw the assent in his girlfriend's eyes. 'Please, that sounds perfect.'

'I get you a beer and I call her. You look thirsty.' The man turned and crossed the dusty road and disappeared behind the curtain of blooms which almost obscured the glass-front to his restaurant.

'I think we made the right choice. I already love it here. I can't remember the last time I was this relaxed.' Isabelle sank back into her chair and Andrew leant across the table and took her hand.

'It is marvellous, isn't it?' Staring out into the bay they could see the boats ferrying tourists back to Elounda from the island of Spinalonga. A sea breeze ruffled the awning under which they sat.

The waiter put down two large beers, the frothy drink making rivers of condensation down the icy sides of the chilled glasses, and said, 'The apartment is free. Now you can relax and enjoy your meal, my aunt says there is no rush, she will be there whenever you arrive or leave the key in the door.'

Few words were spoken between them as both felt the weight of their stressful lives draining away. When their food arrived, they thought there was no way they would be able to eat their way through it: giant pink prawns, crispy kalamari, meaty red mullet, tiger-striped sardines and anchovies burnished in olive oil. They must have been hungrier than they realised as they ate all the delicious seafood before the waiter brought them a plate of grapes, apple and water-melon and a small carafe of raki. Sitting down, he introduced himself as Minos, filling the small glasses with the fiery liquid and raising a toast of '*Yamas!*' before giving them directions to his aunt's house.

Leaving the coast, they drove up the steep mountain road the short distance to the village of Epano Elounda. Following Minos' directions they easily found the house where his aunt was waiting to welcome them. She showed them into the first-floor apartment, simply furnished with a bed, wardrobe, table and chairs, a shower room and a small kitchen area equipped with a fridge and gas ring. Opening a door, she led them out onto a terrace. Looking down the mountainside, what they saw took their breath away. Beyond the white village houses, waves of olive trees cascaded down to the sea which glistened in the evening sunshine. They could see all the way to the canal and to the bay of Mirabello in the distance. Andrew reached out and touched Isabelle's hand; turning towards each other, they both smiled.

Over the following days they grew to adore the island and, what had been a passionate relationship developed into love. For both of them, Crete felt like a home. A refuge from the traumatic times their respective lives had brought them to. It was from that day on the terrace in Epano Elounda that they began to dream of a life on the island.

*

In the few years that followed, their love for each other and desire to build a future together did not diminish. Isabelle's work at the refugee camp continued, while Andrew was sent by his newspaper to troubled spots around the world. Whenever their busy schedules allowed, they would escape to Crete to seek the healing their souls needed to be able to continue with their work. There they could relax and find the peace they increasingly craved.

Each time they returned to the island they rented the room in the village from Minos' aunt. While there, they found themselves looking in estate agents' windows and when they were alone they looked at houses for sale on the internet. Each time they visited the island it became harder and harder to leave. They were both dedicated to their professions, but Andrew was exhausted by the travelling and the rootless nature of his existence. Isabelle longed for children and was acutely aware that, in her late thirties, time was not on her side and her job was incompatible with looking after a baby.

But it was not in an estate agent's window or on the internet that they found the house they were to buy. Three years after that first visit, they were walking around the upper reaches of the village when they heard a high-pitched yelping coming from a plot of overgrown land. Isabelle was keen to investigate and, climbing over a low stone wall, they pushed their way through the tussle of shrubs and weeds in the direction of the sound. Bending back stems and branches they helped each other through the jungle of plants. Invisible from the road, the tangled wasteland hid a dilapidated house. A wall sprouting shrubs from between the stones surrounded what could be made out as a terrace. In the shade of the house, a litter of four puppies lay suckling from their mother.

'Poor thing, she looks half starved,' said Isabelle, slowly approaching the exhausted large black dog, who looked not unlike a Labrador.

'Be careful, she might be protective if she's nursing her babies,' Andrew warned.

'She looks too tired to do anything much. We must get her some food and something to drink.' Isabelle looked concerned.

'I'll head back and see what we've got in the apartment, then we can bring back some food from the shops in Elounda later. You stay here, I won't be long.' Andrew turned and made his way back through the undergrowth. Emerging at the boundary wall he stopped, overwhelmed by what confronted him. From this point above Epano Elounda he could see the rooftops of the village houses and the olive groves and wildflower meadows which reached all the way to the bay of Korfos. Turning and looking up he could see the stark ridges of the mountains which cradled the village like an amphitheatre.

It took him minutes to reach the apartment and get a couple of dishes, a bottle of water and some sliced ham from the fridge before making his way back to the house where Isabelle waited with the dog and her puppies. Andrew filled one plate with the ham and another with water, putting them down by the dog's head. The exhausted mother half stood, gently displacing the suckling pups, first emptying the water before ravenously turning to the food.

'She's starving, poor thing,' said Isabelle.

Andrew poured another bowl of water. 'We'll come back later with some dog food and biscuits for her.'

As the dog lay back down, a single wag of her tail told the couple the food and drink they had provided was welcome. Isabelle stroked the dog's head and Andrew looked around at the house which had been hidden from the world for so long. The door from the terrace to the interior was hanging off its hinges and climbing plants covered the lintel and were already encroaching inside. Getting up, he crossed the terrace to the door and forced it further open to look inside. On the faded, flaking blue paint of the door was something daubed in Greek, beneath which in smaller writing were the words 'For Sale' in English, underneath which was a phone number.

Taking out his phone, Andrew made a note of the number. He returned to where Isabelle was still preoccupied with the mother and puppies.

'Look, I've something to show you.' Taking her hand, he led her back through the overgrown garden to the boundary wall. When she emerged from the undergrowth Andrew could see on his girlfriend's face that she was as enchanted as he had been by what she saw.

'And do you know the best thing? It's for sale.' Andrew was unsure what Isabelle would think about what he was suggesting.

'Let's go back and look inside,' Isabelle said, and enthusiastically turned and headed towards the house.

Underneath the plants which crept up the walls and across the windows the white paint was tired and dirty, and blue shutters hung from the window frames, but the walls looked sturdy and sound. The couple squeezed through the door and a lizard scuttled past. Inside, cobwebs hung from every wall and in the darkness it was hard to see. Andrew forced open the two ground floor windows and the light revealed a large room with a brick fireplace adjoined to a small kitchen area and a bathroom. Andrew flicked a switch but there was no electricity; turning on a tap, his suspicions were confirmed as it ran dry.

'It's just perfect,' Andrew heard Isabelle mutter wistfully.

'Yes it is, isn't it?' he whispered in reply.

Upstairs were two bedrooms in a similar condition, and a door leading out onto another terrace filled with containers full of dead plants, the floor tiles invisible under layers of mud and dust. From here they could look out across the overgrown garden and the panorama was even more breathtaking than the one from the boundary wall.

That evening they returned to the house, trying not to trip over the roots of the unruly plants as the light faded. The dog still lay on the terrace but wagged her tail, pleased to see them, and happy for the food they had brought her, eating hungrily as her pups snuggled by her side. Andrew was pleased they had a torch as darkness came quickly. Finding their way back through the undergrowth, they headed for the village taverna and, tucking into plates of mezzes and a carafe of wine, spoke enthusiastically about buying the house. Andrew thought that he could cope with the restoration of the building, cleaning, sanding, painting and fixing doors and windows, but it was the garden that had caught Isabelle's imagination.

She loved being outdoors and, looking back, remembered how she had escaped into her parents' well-tended plot at her childhood home in Devon. Suddenly she was overwhelmed by memories of those happy days of her youth when her day-to-day life was not dominated by suffering. As Andrew talked, she felt her mind drifting and tears running down her cheeks before dropping on the paper tablecloth. Andrew took her hand.

'Come on, let's get back.' Turning in his chair he signalled for the bill.

'*Avrio*, tomorrow,' the owner mouthed. Andrew put his arm around Isabelle and pressed her to him as they walked up the dark village lane back to their room.

Once they were inside, he ushered her out onto the terrace. 'I'll make us a coffee.' He pulled up two chairs and helped Isabelle into one.

'I'm sorry. I don't know what came over me.' Isabelle wiped a bare arm across her eyes.

'Don't apologise. I'll get those coffees and if you feel like it you can talk about it.'

Left alone, Isabelle stared down the mountainside at the lights of Elounda mimicking the stars which glittered above. She could make out a lone caique puttering across the bay. She tried to gather her thoughts.

When Andrew returned with the coffees they sat and talked. It was as though a switch had been flicked inside Isabelle and all the pent-up emotions of the worries of her work and her longing to have a child gushed out of her. Something about the old house and the thought of creating a garden had touched her soul. She had never felt more relaxed than she was on Crete with Andrew. Now that the possibility of making a home in the village had taken on a tangible form, she took her reaction to it as a sign.

Through the years of working as a doctor in disaster zones, she had always loved being able to help people; so the anxiety that had suddenly gripped her had come as a shock. It seemed the pressures of her job were beginning to get to her. She felt as though she was falling into an abyss of fear and the thought of having a home here was something to hold on to. As they talked about the house, her fear began to subside. Could they make a future for themselves in the village? Andrew admitted that he too was struggling with the dangers and uncertainty of his work, and had ambitions to write a book. Working abroad with their accommodation provided had enabled them both to save some money. If the house was not expensive they should have enough left over to survive on until Andrew could establish himself as a writer. They decided that they would make enquiries. The very thought of moving to the village both excited them and worked as a balm on the anxiety which had welled up inside Isabelle.

The next day Andrew rang the number painted on the door and, after some negotiation with the agent, he managed to agree a price that they could afford. On the recommendation of the owner of the taverna, they found a solicitor in Agios Nikolaos to handle the purchase. She took them to the notary to sign papers and to the bank to open an account before reassuring them that she would deal with everything else.

In just a couple of months they got word that they were owners of the house. The news made the change to their lives very real. Both of them rather nervously tendered their resignations and began to serve their respective periods of notice. They decided to spend that Christmas in England, seeing family and friends before flying out to Athens and taking a ferry to Crete. The January day they approached the island it was calm, warm and bright and for the first few weeks the couple worked tirelessly cleaning, painting, hammering and doing all that they could to make their house habitable before they could start the serious renovations. The winter days were full of sunshine which was reflected in the couple's optimism as they began to forge their new home. Andrew had tied a brush to a pole and swept the chimney and, in the cold evenings, the couple would snuggle together in front of a fire fuelled by wood gathered from the overgrown garden.

But as the weeks wore on, it became impossible to ignore news of the pandemic which was spreading through Europe and already had reached the UK. When they went into Elounda for supplies, the streets were almost deserted and face masks were being worn by the few people who did venture out. In the tavernas which opened, talk was of little else but the killer virus. Andrew could see that his girlfriend was wrestling with her conscience. When she told him she was returning to England to work in the fight to control the disease, he was unable to stop her.

'I have to go and help out. It won't be for long. You stay and make a start on fixing up the house.' For Isabelle, there was no way she could not have responded to the call for doctors to help in hospitals in the UK. She was still young and healthy and had only just given up her job with Médecins Sans Frontières to build a new life with Andrew. After all, it was only to be for a few months at the most and he had plenty to do on the house.

Andrew spent his days doing bits and bobs around the house but somehow, without Isabelle by his side, he lacked the motivation he so recently had felt. He loved being on the island but, without his girlfriend, the sun had lost some of its sparkle and the scents of the sea and the mountain herbs had somehow been dulled. They talked by phone whenever Isabelle could grab a moment away from the wards. After they had spoken Andrew regained some of his enthusiasm, but found this draining away until he heard from her again.

*

Andrew's life had changed forever. A phone call from a hospital in Birmingham had rendered him numb, unable to move from the step where he sat. The possibilities that moments before he had been looking forward to, now did not register. His eyes were full of tears and his mind unable to take in the enormity of the news. For what seemed like hours he remained rooted to the spot, unable to see further than the overgrown garden. Beyond the tangle of weeds were the olive groves sweeping down to the bay below, the view which had led him and Isabelle to buy the house. Now the dream of a future here was in tatters.

As a journalist, Andrew had been in many situations that had frightened him. He had been on assignments to war zones and disasters all over the world but he had always managed to find some emotional response which allowed him to cope. Now he struggled to find anything to cling on to. Why had he let Isabelle return to England? Had he been in a more rational state he would have known the answer. He could not have stopped her, and that was one of the reasons why he loved her. They had been that close to achieving their dream. Now that had been snatched away by the killer virus that was sweeping the world.

Andrew didn't know how long he sat outside. At first, he was stunned. Then the tears came before the pain wracked his whole body. For what seemed like an eternity he felt as though he could not contain the agony and anger that had taken him over. When exhaustion relieved him of the physical torment he was cut adrift, his mind unable to find an anchorage.

It was so unfair. Isabelle had been young and fit. She had told him about shortages of personal protective equipment in the hospitals but had always been upbeat when she had spoken to him on the phone. Even when he found out she had contracted the disease, he had been confident she would pull through.

The end had come so quickly and he had not had the chance to say goodbye to the woman he loved more than anything else in the world. He had never felt so alone. He sensed something on his knee, and looking down he saw the dog they had fed all those months ago resting her head on him. He reached out and stroked her; she did not move and Andrew felt the grief flooding through him again.

As darkness fell he had not moved from his spot on the terrace with the dog by his side. He felt no hunger or thirst but, exhausted, knew he must sleep. Something inside told him to get some food for the dog and he put a plate of ham from the fridge on the kitchen floor before collapsing into bed. Drained, his body would not succumb to the exhaustion that gripped him. At some time he must have slipped into a dreamless sleep, awaking to the sound of a cockerel crowing and light seeping in through the unshuttered windows. As his thoughts reformed, the reality of Isabelle's death hit him again, leaving him numb. He reached out an arm, knowing she would never be there again. He felt the dog lick his outstretched hand.

And Life Goes On

2013-2020

AFTER THE INITIAL sadness about the demise of her relationship with Nick, Amy had surprised herself by how she had managed to get over his leaving. On the drive back from Sougia the conversation in the minibus had been polite but forced, Amy and Nick unsure of what to say to one another, and the other members of the walking society embarrassed after the events of the previous evening. When they got back to Epano Elounda, it was conspicuous that Nick had dropped Amy off first, beside the church of Zoodoho Pigi. Amy had turned to wave goodbye as she reached the overgrown path which led into the village, but Nick had already pulled away.

The society continued to meet weekly in the village taverna, and regularly met up for walks at the weekends. Nick was never mentioned again by the group, at least in earshot of Amy and, as the months went by her ex-boyfriend entered her thoughts less and less. In the early days after the split, if she did need to open up to anyone, Amy would talk to Suzi and Stelios to whom she had grown particularly close. Since they had first met they had felt at ease with the easy-going, blonde English woman whose relaxed manner was in such contrast with their more serious outlooks on life. When they had married, Amy had been invited to the wedding. As a present she gave them a large abstract landscape she had painted of Spinalonga. The painting now took pride of place in the waiting room of Stelios' surgery in Elounda where the couple lived in the upstairs apartment.

Suzi's fledgling practice was near the lake in Agios Nikolaos and the lawyer was always happy to help Amy on the occasions she had to navigate her way through the mire of official bureaucracy, never accepting any payment from her friend. Over the years, the couple tried to set Amy up on dates with other friends. These occasionally resulted in a brief fling, but it seemed that Amy was too protective of her freedom to commit to a lasting relationship. She was at her most content when painting or walking in the hills or by the sea.

In her friendships with Suzi and Stelios, other members of the walking society and the villagers she had everything she wanted. She was happy to be independent and any dreams she had were of new pictures to paint or walks to discover. Her canvasses were getting bigger and she applied the paint with decorator's brushes and large palette knives, her broad strokes laying deep textures on the surface. She longed to take on the challenge of scaling the island's greatest peaks, particularly Mount Ida in the Psiloritis mountain range, but each year, for one reason or another, the narrow window of time when the group could make the climb passed them by.

Amy would dutifully call her mother on a regular basis, but their conversations were short and muted, Amy unable to articulate to her mother the joy she felt in the life she was living, and her mother unable to forgive her daughter for deserting her all those years before. Reconciliation was something for another day, sometime in the future.

Every couple of years Amy would fly to the UK to visit her mother and her sister but she dreaded going there. The cold politeness of her relationship with her mum, and the sadness she felt at how her sister had been changed by her marriage to the pompous snob Nigel made her visits a chore, and she had lost all contact with her father. She loved her niece Alice but with each visit noticed how she was becoming spoiled and joyless.

From the moment her plane touched down in London she would long to return to the village. Even as she passed through airport security on her way back to Crete she felt an immense sense of relief to be going home. She was at ease in her house in the village, in its comfortable disarray. She loved the smell of the paint, linseed oil and turpentine in her chaotic studio, and the terrace redolent with the flowers and herbs she lovingly tended in an array of pots and planters.

Invitations to exhibit her work were growing more frequent, keeping Amy busy creating new works which would be sold at her shows. One large painting on an easel in the studio had remained there for a number of years, a work in progress. It was a multiple canvas picture of the neighbouring property, depicting the ongoing encroachment of the small house which lay at the heart of its wild garden. When Amy was not working on paintings for exhibitions or smaller works to sell in local shops, she would carry the easel out onto the terrace and resume her visual documentation of the passing of time on the cottage next door.

Mostly her days were not planned. Apart from commitments to exhibit her paintings, she could spend her days doing much as she pleased, working, reading, swimming, meeting with friends or exploring with the walking society.

When the pandemic struck and she was forced into lockdown, at first Amy felt anxious about the uncertainties that came with it. She would search for news on the internet but soon realised that this made the situation more worrying, so rationed herself to reading one short update daily. She hated the restrictions the regulations imposed on the serendipitous nature of her life but realised how lucky she was to have her painting. She would speak to her friends on the phone regularly, and enjoyed the days when she would get a pass to walk down the track to go shopping in Elounda. The thing she missed most was being able to meet up with the other members of the walking society and freedom of their walks together.

These days the usually quiet lanes were mostly deserted, the villagers kept at home by strict laws imposed on them by their leaders and their anxieties about the pandemic. It had been several weeks since Amy had heard the rumour that the couple who came each year to holiday in the village had bought the ramshackle house next to hers. Over recent years she had occasionally seen them in the village and greeted them with a smile or the occasional '*kalimera*'. Now the couple were neighbours, she decided to make an effort to introduce herself. She would have liked to have invited them around to her house for a drink, but the covid restrictions made that impossible.

By now Amy had got used to the enforced isolation. She spent the time painting and reading. She was pleased that she did not have a television to fuel any fears and frustrations deep within her. How would her neighbours be coping just having moved here, probably not knowing anyone and being unfamiliar with all the new, ever-changing, regulations?

That morning she needed to go down into Elounda to stock up on groceries and decided to offer to do some shopping for the new arrivals as a way of introducing herself. That must be allowed, she thought. Amy texted the code to get her permission to go out to shop. Putting on her face mask and grabbing her shopping bags, she headed outside. She walked along the stone wall to where a hole had been cut in the vegetation to reveal a broken gate jammed open to allow access. The tangle of plants blocked out the spring sunshine and exuded a sense of foreboding, but something drew her in.

Stepping through the gap, she brushed aside the low-hanging branches and edged her way towards the house. A dog barked, and what she thought might be a black Labrador pushed its way through the undergrowth and sat in front of Amy, barring her way. She might have been intimidated but the slow sweep of the dog's tail across the path revealed its true nature. Stepping forward, she held out her hand for it to sniff. The dog gave up any pretence of being a barrier to her progress by giving her a lick. Turning, it led her along a path that had been roughly hewn through the overgrown garden.

Awake on his bed, tormented and immobilised by the news of Isabelle's death, Andrew heard a guttural, melodic howl preceding a knock on the open front door.

'Hello, is there anyone at home?'

Andrew raised himself from the bed and willed himself in the direction of the door where a woman stood smiling. He vaguely recognised her as someone from the village.

'I came to ask if I could pick you up any shopping. I'm Amy, from next door.' Her words tailed off as the light caught her neighbour's face. 'Perhaps now isn't a good time?'

The man in front of her was ashen and drawn and looked as though he was straining every sinew just to stand upright.

'Are you OK? Can I get you some help?' Amy took a step across the threshold towards him. This was not the cheerful, confident man she had greeted as he walked with his girlfriend through the village.

'No, I'll be alright.' Part of Andrew wanted nothing more than for this woman to go away, but from somewhere deep in himself he felt the urge to tell someone of his misery. He was alone here now; alone in the village and alone in the world. His past was too painful to remember and his future had been shattered. All he was aware of now was the nothingness which surrounded him as he stood talking to a woman he didn't know. He felt the cool of the stone floor beneath his feet and as his sight cleared he could see the concerned smile of his neighbour looking at him. From nowhere he heard himself saying, 'She's dead. Isabelle's dead.'

Stepping forward, Amy instinctively put her arms around him. As he bent his head into her shoulder, she could feel the damp of his silent tears soaking through her top. She did not know how long they stood there in the half light of the old cottage. She did not ask any questions of him as he clung to her as though she was the only thing that could stop him from sinking.

When it seemed as though he had no more tears to shed, Andrew released his grip. 'I'm sorry.' He took a step back. He could see the worry on her kind face, the wrinkles across her forehead and the moisture in her deep blue eyes and the stain of his tears on her white cotton blouse.

'Don't apologise. Shall I make us some coffee?' Not waiting for an answer, Amy put her shopping bag down on the rickety table next to the small work surface that served as a kitchen. She filled the kettle and switched it on, spooning coffee from the open foil packet into a coffee press and taking two mugs from a shelf above the sink. She turned and almost fell over the dog which was sitting and looking up to her with doe eyes, her tail beating out a slow rhythm on the stone floor. She bent and stroked her head.

'She seems to have adopted me. She adored Isabelle.'

Amy poured water into the press. 'Do you take milk or sugar?' she asked.

'No, neither. There's sugar in the cupboard if you like it but I haven't any milk.'

'Black's fine for me.' Amy pushed down the filter and poured the coffee. 'Shall we sit outside?'

Amy carried the mugs towards the rectangle of light and out into the small clearing outside the cottage door, placing the coffees down on a rusty, round metal table. The dog followed her outside, Andrew stepping out last into the dappled shade. She pulled up one of two rushwork chairs for him before sitting on the other. The dog flopped down on the ground, her head gently resting on Amy's foot.

'Do you want to talk?'

Amy left the question hanging in the air, and her silence gave Andrew the chance to grasp it. He did not know where to start, but knew he should fill the void or he might be lost. He started hesitatingly, each step of the story punctuated by waves of despair. Talking to a stranger about his innermost feelings felt strange, but as he went on Andrew couldn't stop himself from pouring out his raw emotions.

He told Amy how his girlfriend had returned to England to work as a doctor in the frontline fight against the coronavirus. How he loved her for that but hated himself for not fighting harder for her to stay with him on Crete. He spoke of their dreams for her to make a garden and him to write a book, and their hopes that in settling on the island they could leave the stresses of their past behind them.

Amy let Andrew talk, his words a jumble of self-recrimination and remorse. Somehow he could not find the chink in his anguish which would allow him some comfort. Amy knew it would take time, that just being there listening, she was helping to let the pain flow out from this broken man. Eventually the outpourings slowed to a trickle and the tears dried.

Andrew's throat felt parched. Exhausted by grief, he had no more tears to shed. To divert attention from the pain, his racing mind turned to the practicalities. The doctor who had phoned to tell Andrew of Isabelle's passing had also informed Isabelle's parents as they were registered as her next of kin. He had not spoken to them about arrangements for the funeral or registering the death. Somehow he had to find the strength to make contact.

Andrew's relationship with his girlfriend's parents had always been fragile, he explained to Amy. They had resented her dangerous work abroad and although her choice of career had nothing to do with Andrew, they blamed him for her not returning to live near them. They had hoped that when she had come to her senses she would move back to England. When she had told them she was moving to Crete they were distraught, blaming Andrew for stealing their daughter from them. But in the end it had been returning to England that had killed her.

Amy offered to stay whilst he made the call. Taking a deep breath, Andrew punched in the number on his phone. It appeared the line was busy and Amy could see he was losing his resolve as he tried again and again.

'Hello.' At last Andrew got through. 'I'm so sorry…' As soon as Andrew began to speak he was cut short and Amy could see the look of shock on his face, followed by anger and then despair. Before he had been able to say another word he was staring at the phone. Isabelle's father had hung up on him.

For what seemed like minutes Andrew sat frozen in disbelief before Amy broke the silence to ask what had happened. His face flushed with anger, Andrew explained that Isabelle's father had told him that he had already arranged a funeral and due to restricted numbers at the crematorium he was not welcome, even if he could find a flight to return. Andrew was not sure whether or not to believe his dead girlfriend's father, or indeed whether he would be allowed to fly to England. But either way it was clear he was not wanted at Isabelle's funeral.

Andrew felt hopeless and helpless. The distress now mingled with rage and guilt in a toxic mix which threatened to envelop him. His fists bunched tight he headed towards the trees before turning and walking inside the cottage and then back to the terrace. He could not sit, but every time he entered the house, memories of his dead girlfriend assailed him. Outside, the overgrown patch of land reminded him of Isabelle's dream of making a garden here in the place they had hoped to start a family. Nowhere that he turned could he find solace.

Amy struggled to find words to soothe him as he wrestled with the pain inside. She recognised that there was nothing she could say at that moment which could change the way he felt, but knew at some stage he would need to reconnect with the mundane needs of everyday life. She looked at her watch. The pass that had been sent to her mobile phone to come out of isolation to shop had long expired.

'Can I make you another coffee?' Amy asked, as the words came out she sensed how lame the offer must sound, but it was the best she could do.

'Thank you,' Andrew replied without looking around.

Whilst inside, Amy looked in the fridge. There was an open packet of feta cheese, butter, two tomatoes, four tins of beer and a bottle of wine. The kitchen cupboard revealed little more: some biscuits, an open packet of pasta, honey and an unopened jar of olives.

'I'll be going down to do some shopping tomorrow; can I get some food in for you?' Amy asked, carrying the two mugs out and putting them down. 'I was going today but I'm a bit late now. I've got some bits at home that will do for lunch and dinner today.'

Despite not having eaten since the previous afternoon, he had no appetite but realised he would need to eat. Neither was he sure that he wanted to be alone. 'That's very kind of you. Would you like to join me?' As the words came out, Andrew was embarrassed that he might have sounded needy. Why would this complete stranger want to spend time with a person she didn't know and who was in the depths of despair?

'Thank you, that's kind,' Amy replied, smiling. 'After I've drunk my coffee I'll go back to mine and see what I can rustle up.'

Back at home, Amy filled a carrier bag with the ingredients to make a salad for lunch and half a loaf of bread; she took some pork chops from the freezer and potatoes from a cupboard. She was unsure what the regulations were regarding mixing with a person so obviously in need. Any fears she had of the virus were put aside in order to do whatever was necessary to help her distraught neighbour. Pushing through the shrubs next door she saw Andrew sitting, staring into the distance, the dog beside him. But on the table he had put out some oil and vinegar, cutlery and two tumblers.

In the kitchen she chopped tomatoes and a cucumber before slicing an onion and adding feta cheese and dressing the salad in oil and vinegar. She cut some slices from yesterday's loaf and sprinkled it with olive oil to make it more palatable. As Amy took out the salad, Andrew stood and went inside to the fridge, returning with a bottle of wine. Without a word he opened it and poured them both a glass.

That afternoon the pair sat mostly in silence, he unable to find the words to talk and she allowing him the space to discover them. At dinnertime she cooked the chops and they ate watching the sun dropping down behind the mountains above the house. It was dark when Amy stood to leave.

'Thank you,' Andrew said as she picked up her bag.

'Try to get some sleep. I'll go shopping early tomorrow and drop it off when I get back.' Amy turned and made for the gap through the shrubs.

'Goodnight,' Andrew whispered. She turned. 'Goodnight, Andrew.' With that she left him, his hand on the big black dog which was resting her head on his knee.

The following day Amy returned with a bag full of supplies to fill up Andrew's empty fridge and cupboards. The tiredness which inhabited his body showed on his face and in the heaviness of his limbs, but from somewhere he had found a voice to express his desolation. Amy listened, providing words of comfort when she thought they were needed but letting her new friend find a way to exorcise his sorrow.

Over the days and weeks that followed, Amy visited regularly. The enormity of Andrew's heartbreak and her need to console him formed a bubble around them and most of the time banished concerns of the pandemic raging in the outside world which might otherwise have overwhelmed them. Slowly she noticed her neighbour finding acceptance of the loss he so keenly felt. Little by little Amy began to discern his thoughts turning to a future in which he would have to live without Isabelle.

Rebuilding the Dream

2020–2021

AT FIRST ANDREW struggled to see anything apart from the sadness which engulfed him. As time went by the anguish was diluted, and haltingly his mind opened up chinks where thoughts about the future crept in. There was nothing for him back in England, no house, no job; his father had died five years earlier and his mother had moved in with his brother and sister-in-law. Every time he thought of the possibility of moving back there he felt his mood plummet, his mind fogged with memories of Isabelle's death, her father's bitterness and the all-encompassing miasma of the virus. He had little need for other people, he was self-contained. He had spent the latter part of his life travelling around the world alone.

Some months after Isabelle had died he awoke early, the sun already up as he pulled on his jeans. Something was missing. Usually as soon as he stirred the dog would stand and lick his face as he lay in bed. This morning there was no sign of her. He pulled on a shirt, slipped into his shoes and made for the front door. As he emerged into the light he saw the dog sitting facing him. He reached down to stroke her head and the dog turned and took a few steps in the direction of the undergrowth and sat again.

He moved towards her, and she stood up and disappeared down the path through the tangle of plants. She had been with him through all his desolation and he had not even given her a name. That had been something the couple had been planning to do together when Isabelle returned from England. Ducking under the branches he followed her through the morass; she deserved a walk, at least.

The view at the end of the path startled him. The dog stood on her back legs, her front paws resting on a fallen section of the dry stone wall. Andrew felt his breathing grow shallower and speed up, and his head went light. He was taken back to the first time he had looked from here down the olive-covered mountainside to the bay. It was this that had first made them fall in love with the old house. He sat on the wall and took in the panorama as he had that day when they discovered the cottage. A tear ran down his cheek. He wiped it away with his hand. The dog rested her head on Andrew's knee and instinctively he reached down and stroked her.

From somewhere, light managed to penetrate his soul, a glimmer of hope for the future which he had not felt since Isabelle's death. There was not a breath of wind and the cicadas had not yet warmed to their daily chorus. He stared out at the olive groves, down to the sugar-cube houses of Elounda and past the canal to the bay of Mirabello.

In that moment, Andrew decided two things. He would stay here in the house, and the dog would be called Bella. He tried the name, and the dog licked his hand. He stood and thought about going for a walk, then remembered he needed to text for permission to leave his home. Turning, he made his way back along the path through the undergrowth towards the house. 'Bella,' he called and she followed him back to the terrace.

When Amy arrived for her daily visit she was happy to see Andrew sitting with the dog beside him, the hint of a smile in his eyes. Something had changed. Had he managed to find something positive that he could cling to and drag himself out of his despair?

As Amy did every day, she went inside and made them a coffee, but when she sat back down, instead of sitting in silence as they usually did, Andrew began to talk. He told Amy how he had named the dog, and that he had decided to stay on in the house and make his life there. He wanted to clear the trees and tangle of weeds so he could look down to the sea and make a garden in memory of Isabelle. Then maybe he would turn his attentions to restoring the cottage and at some time realise his dream of writing a book.

Amy was delighted at the turn of events but knew that this was only the beginning of his coming to terms with the loss of Isabelle. There would be many lows ahead, but this was a start. She suggested he make a plan for the garden and a list of things he would need to begin the work. Enthusiastically he got a notebook and pencil and sat down to write. Almost immediately Amy saw a cloud of despondence drift over his expression as the scale of the task dawned on him.

'I don't mind giving you a hand if you think I'd be of any use,' she offered.

Lifting his head, Andrew smiled. 'I'd like that, if you can spare the time.'

'Time is something we all have rather a lot of at the moment.' Amy laughed. 'First of all we will need some tools: a saw, loppers, shears, a spade and rake. We can get them all from the hardware shop in Elounda. It will take some time to clear all this and burn the waste, then we can start planning for the new garden. Hopefully when we have got that far it will be easier to get out and about and we can explore some garden centres to find plants.'

Amy's enthusiasm seemed to buoy Andrew up. He was not even deterred when Amy told him that the house had been uninhabited and the garden untended since long before she had bought her home in the village. He jotted down a list of the equipment they needed to get started on the job. It was decided that the following day he would get a covid text code to go shopping and walk down the donkey track to the hardware store to get the tools.

When Amy arrived to begin work the following morning, Andrew had already returned with his purchases: a large bow saw, secateurs, extendable loppers and a garden spade.

'I couldn't carry any more up the hill, but this should do to make a start. I can go back to get a rake and anything else we need another day.'

Amy went inside to make a coffee, and she could see by the speed at which Andrew drank his that he was keen to get started. They decided to begin clearing the terrace area outside the front door and work outwards towards the wall. Andrew grabbed the saw and headed for a sturdy shrub growing out of the dry earth beside the narrow path.

'I think we might want to work out what to cut down first, what to try and dig out and move, and what to just prune. I don't know much about gardens, but some of these plants we might be able to use elsewhere,' said Amy.

'Do you know what they all are?' Andrew asked.

'Some, not all, but I have an app on my phone which will tell us if I take a picture, then we can research them online.'

Amy could see Andrew wanted to get straight to work. She didn't want to curb any of his enthusiasm as she knew the challenge of creating the garden would keep his mind from wandering back to the dark place it had been for months. 'Why don't I do the research and label the plants telling us which to cut down, dig up or leave, and you can do the hard labour?' Amy suggested.

And hard labour it was in the summer heat. The parched earth was rock solid and digging was arduous, but while he was working Andrew was distracted from thoughts of Isabelle. When memories of her entered his mind he took comfort knowing the garden they were making was in remembrance of the woman he had loved. Not only was the work a diversion from the sadness but each day

Andrew got fitter, his lean body more tanned and his lengthening hair grew lighter in the burning sunshine.

Amy would get up early and work on her paintings outside on her terrace in the first light of morning. Unable to sell her work or exhibit during the pandemic, she was happy to spend much of her day helping her neighbour.

The work was slow and painstaking, but Andrew was grateful for Amy's methodical approach. As the weeks wore on, he started to take an interest in the plants and engage with Amy's thoughts about how they could shape the design, and the colours that would adorn the space.

The sweat poured off him as he dug deep to uproot a rogue fig tree which they had decided to move to the edge of the plot. Exhausted and flushed with success, Andrew felt a sense of achievement at his labours. Every day he got stronger in mind and body. Each evening they would sit down with Bella at their feet and drink a glass of wine and plan the following day's work. Amy would show him watercolour sketches of ideas for the finished garden. Andrew marvelled at the paintings, which inspired him to carry on with the heavy labour.

*

Autumn was approaching by the time the ground was cleared, and one day in October, after their work was done, they sat down and looked at the view. Beyond the perimeter of the garden they could see the tops of olive trees and the sky, but because the terrace was set back close to the house, they could not see down the mountainside to the sea.

Amy could sense that Andrew's pleasure at having finished the heavy work of clearing the plot was tinged with disappointment that he couldn't see the bay from the terrace. Reaching into her tote bag she pulled out her sketch pad and began to draw.

As Andrew leaned over to see what she was drawing she snatched the pad away. 'No don't look yet! I'm just putting some thoughts down on paper.'

'I'll go and get the drinks then.' Andrew stood and made for the door of the cottage.

'Could you bring me a glass of water for the paints?' Amy asked as he disappeared inside.

With drinks in front of them, they sat in silence, Amy absorbed in her plan for the garden and Andrew impatient to see what she had sketched. Using her small travel tin of paints, she washed tints over her pencil lines and then added detail in dots of bright, vivid colour. When she was satisfied with her work she put the pad down on the table and slid it across to Andrew.

It took a moment for him to orientate himself then a second more to say 'Wow, that's beautiful!'

Amy had sketched a second terrace beside the dry-stone wall where it bordered the narrow track which led to the front of the property. The new terrace would be reached by a path bordered with trees from the patio where they now sat, which in the watercolour was shaded by a pergola attached to the house wall and draped in purple bougainvillea. Around both terraces were terracotta pots and pithoi radiant with blooms of every hue.

'I love it.' Andrew rose from his seat and walked round the table and gave Amy a hug.

'It'll be a lot of work.' Amy brought her friend back down to earth. 'And will take a long time.'

'That's not the biggest problem at the moment,' he replied. 'It will be getting hold of the stone, wood and other building materials.'

'I think we might be in luck if we order online. Tomorrow we can measure up and work out what we need, then we can mark out the plot and try to get the materials delivered.'

The following day the ordering was a success, but the trucks to bring the materials would be too big to get close to the house. Andrew bought a wheelbarrow from the hardware store and wheeled it up the donkey track in preparation for the delivery.

The hardcore and stone to lay the new terrace were dumped by the roadside along with bags of cement, concrete and sand, later to be joined by the wood for the pergola. Dripping with sweat, Andrew wheeled the stones one by one up the narrow road which led to the house and unloaded them in a pile on the other side of the dry-stone wall. Amy helped by carrying the lighter bits of timber and getting cold drinks from the fridge in the kitchen. Although the work was backbreaking for Andrew, she was pleased to see that he never wavered in his determination to finish the task. It took until the middle of the afternoon before the last stone was added to the pile and Andrew slumped exhausted into his chair outside the house.

'I'll get us a beer,' said Amy heading indoors.

'I'll just have a water, please,' replied Andrew. 'If I have a drink I might nod off and I want to make a start laying the base for the stones.'

It was all Amy could do to persuade him to stop working for the day. She could tell that he was exhausted and was worried that, although making the garden was helping heal, it might become dangerously obsessive.

Accepting the beer Amy offered him, he relaxed and any strength that might have remained drained from his body as they made plans for the following day's work. When Amy left for home, Andrew fell into bed and slept from the early evening until the next day. His sleep was untroubled by dreams, and he awoke to the sound of Amy knocking on the half-open door. Blinking himself awake, he realised that he was still wearing the clothes he had worn the previous day and was ravenous as he had not eaten.

'You get a shower, and I'll make us some food.' Amy placed a carrier bag on the kitchen table and pulled out eggs, a pack of bacon, some tomatoes, mushrooms and bread. 'I thought you might be hungry after all your hard work, so I popped down to Elounda for some shopping.'

Andrew ate the breakfast and although his body still ached from the previous day's exertions, he was keen to get started laying the new terrace.

'Go on then, you get to work while I clear away the plates,' Amy said, laughing.

Picking up the spade propped against the house, Andrew made his way to the plot beside the stone wall which he had marked out with pegs and string. He was eager to prepare the ground but as he became absorbed in the work, found the patience he needed to do the job perfectly. Using a spirit level, he got the hardcore as even as was possible before mixing the first bag of concrete. He realised he could only put down small amounts of the mix as in the sun it would dry out in no time.

It was dusk when Andrew had levelled the last load of concrete and stood back to admire his work. His body was aching but he smiled at the progress he had made. Walking back towards the house he could see that Amy had also been busy, digging over the dry earth around the old terrace beside the house.

'I thought you might need this.' Amy put a bottle of beer down on the table. 'Then you'd better get another shower, or you'll be stiff tomorrow. I'll make dinner.'

Preparing the food, Amy pondered how content she had been over the last months helping Andrew. She surprised herself by not resenting the time she had spent away from her painting. Alone at home in the evenings she managed to sketch, and if she was not too tired she would paint. She was pleased that she had been able to help her neighbour when he needed her most and in helping him it seemed she had fulfilled a need in herself that she had not been aware of. There was no doubt that Andrew was handsome but it was his friendship that she valued. She pondered how she had always shied away from commitment to other people and how for the first time since Nick had left for America seven years earlier she had allowed herself to invest part of her life in someone else's. In helping Andrew to rebuild his life, she realised she had enriched her own.

Refreshed, Andrew dressed and returned outside just as Amy was laying the table before bringing out a salad, potatoes roasted in garlic, oil and lemon and grilled pork chops. Both of them were hungrier than they realised and said little until they had taken the edge off their appetites. When they began to engage in conversation the talk was of their plans for the following day. Andrew would start to lay the stones for the new terrace whilst Amy was to replant the shrubs and flowers they had rescued whilst cutting down the undergrowth and plan what new plants they would need to buy to finish the garden.

The next day Andrew began piecing together the stones and cementing them into place. First he had to lay them out and move them around like a jigsaw puzzle to see the best fit. Where he could not find a pattern that pleased him he would split the stones with a hammer and cold chisel until he found the shape he was satisfied with. The going was slow, and by the end of that second day he had only cemented down a small area of stone but he was pleased with his work and happy to take as long as it needed to finish.

Sometimes Amy would watch her friend selecting and offering up the stones before dotting them with cement and taking a rubber mallet to bed them down onto the concrete base. She smiled at how his absorption in the task was helping him heal.

In the weeks Andrew spent laying the terrace by the wall, Amy spent her time bent over her sketchbook, planning the plants that would adorn the garden. She painted the path which ran between the two terraces, shrouded on either side by trees: olive, lemon, fig and pomegranate. As she made her lists she could almost smell the herbs she was proposing to plant in large pithoi outside the door to the house.

As autumn turned into winter, the terrace was complete, and buoyed up with his successful work, Andrew set about the pathway. This was made of smaller stones, and with the experience he had gained laying the terrace, work on this went more quickly. The days were short and mostly crisp and as the year turned he began work on constructing the pergola. Beams were mounted to the side of the house, and uprights bolted to brackets fixed into the old terrace before the cross struts, over which they planned to grow a vine, were screwed together. Andrew surprised himself at his ability to take on the practical tasks involved in the carpentry and hard landscaping, and took pride in the way the garden was progressing. Every day he laboured Andrew grew stronger. Now the building tasks were finished Amy hoped that doing the planting would continue to help him through his grieving. In the back of her mind she held a concern that when he had completed the hard work he might slip back into the pain of his heartbreak.

It was now nearly a year since Isabelle's death. Alone in bed at night, Andrew would often succumb to the melancholy at her loss and what their life could have been. Sometimes he was haunted by thoughts of what she had gone through in her final hours and her courage encouraged him to be brave before the exhaustion of his day's toil would free him from these dark thoughts and deliver him to a dreamless sleep. If he awoke feeling the fog of depression swirling around his head, he forced himself to remember that he was doing this in his girlfriend's memory. Increasingly, however, he found himself waking refreshed and keen to get started creating something with his bare hands.

Amy had rescued some mature trees and shrubs from the old garden which she had planted in a patch of ground in a corner of the plot and watered daily to keep them alive. Now she replanted them beside the path, shielding the house from the narrow road which ran beside the dry-stone wall. One morning they set off in Amy's old jeep to a nursery outside Agios Nikolaos on the road to Kritsa with her list of other plants they wanted. Some were in stock, some needed to be ordered and some were too large to fit in Amy's car but they returned to the village with a boot laden with flowers, pots and compost. The poppies, pelargoniums, bougainvillea, geraniums, grape vine, jasmine and oleander gave them plenty to get on with planting until the delivery van arrived a couple of days later with the more mature trees.

Andrew ran a hose from the kitchen tap through the house and out into the garden to water the soil, which after the spring rains was easily turned over with a spade. He had to go to the hardware shop and buy a pick to dig some of the deeper holes in preparation to plant the trees.

Amy filled the clay pots and urns with grit, soil and compost and already the plants on the two terraces made a magnificent display of colour: the red, pink and white of the geraniums, yellow and blood-coloured poppies and the deep purple bougainvillea set to climb the wall of the house. The grape vine was planted at the base of the pergola and its tendrils were wrapped and wired around a post. The herbs were planted in pithoi on either side of the cottage door, leaving the spring air redolent with the smells of thyme, rosemary and sage.

It was easy to work in the warmth of the spring days, seeing the garden take form around them. On the evening of the third day after the last plants had arrived, Andrew dug the final hole and planted a mature, deep-green myrtle bush into the earth, firming it in with his boot before standing back and looking around him. The garden was astonishing and even at its tender age was budding with potential. Admiring their work, he could feel a tear welling up. Amy slipped an arm around his shoulder and pulled him towards her and hugged him tight.

'I've got something in the fridge for us to celebrate.' Letting go of Andrew, Amy headed inside, returning with a chilled bottle of champagne and two tumblers. 'You open it, and I'll light the lanterns.'

Andrew poured two glasses and followed Amy as she carried a pair of candle lights along the path to the new terrace. She put the lanterns on top of the wall. Both of them looked back to observe the stunning garden they had created.

'Shall we sit here?' Amy walked back to the old terrace and got two chairs. Emerging through the new trees, she could see her friend staring down the mountainside. She placed the chairs by the wall, but Andrew didn't move. Standing beside him, she could see his eyes glistening in the candlelight.

'She'd have loved this,' he whispered.

'Yes, she would.' As they both stared down at the bay below. The light of a single fishing boat drew a slow line across the water beneath the star-studded sky.

'To Isabelle.' Amy gently clinked her glass against Andrew's.

'To Isabelle,' echoed Andrew, 'and thank you. I would never have done it without you.'

Amy felt the warmth of his gratitude as they sat down. She could see on Andrew's face that everything they had achieved in making the garden had helped temper the sadness he felt, but now that it was complete, she was still concerned that the void left could be filled with darkness again.

For minutes they sat, each alone with their own thoughts. Then a quiet, soulful sound penetrated the silence, its long tail tapering off and echoing through the surrounding mountains. Again, this time louder from somewhere they could hear the unmistakeable sound of a bow drawn across a lyra's strings. An unseen smile crossed Amy's face as she knew it must be Alexander. It struck her how happy it made her feel that maybe things were starting to return to some normality and that the taverna must be reopening after months of closure. She thought of meeting with her friends again and then wondered if Andrew might join the village walking society?

'Would you like to eat out tonight?' Not waiting for him to answer, Amy stood and Andrew followed her towards the gate and the sounds of the lyra.

A Chance for Change

2021

NEWS OF THE sudden stroke which had taken her mother's life shook Amy to the core. She had not been close to her for years – really for her whole adult life since she had escaped to Crete. Her visits to see family had always been infused with restrained politeness rather than affection. Somehow, deep down, Amy thought that her mother would always be there and that their fractious relationship was unfinished business, something that could be healed at some point in the future. Knowing that this would no longer be possible left Amy numb.

The phone call had come from her sister as Amy was sitting outside the village taverna with some members of the walking group. Emma sounded hysterical on the other end of the line. Through the tears Amy managed to make out that her sister had called round to visit their mother and found her collapsed on the bathroom floor. She had called an ambulance but it was already too late.

It was clear that Amy must return to England, not only to pay her last respects to her mother but to lend support to Emma who was obviously struggling to cope. Ever since their father had walked out, their mother had been protective towards Emma. The younger sister was everything Amy was not. She had not run away and left. She had grown into the daughter Amy could never have been. She had been dutiful; even when she had gone to university she had come home at weekends. She had married 'well' to a stockbroker in the City and had no need or desire to work, and in happier times Emma would take a weekly drive down from the leafy London suburbs to the Sussex countryside and go to lunch with her mother. Since the pandemic Emma had formed a bubble with her mother, and when possible continued her weekly visits.

Emma had never been to Greece – in fact, she had barely been to Europe. Paris and Barcelona for city breaks was the extent of her experience of the continent. She and her husband preferred to go further afield, to what they considered more exotic locations in the Caribbean or the Far East. The arrival of their only child, Alice, soon after they were married when Emma was twenty-one had not curtailed their holidays. When the child was young she travelled with her nanny and when she was older she was sent away to a boarding school on the south coast of England. Now she was safely away at university, studying for a degree in business management.

Whenever Amy was back in England, she would visit the detached mock-Georgian house in Surrey to see her sister, although she could always feel the distain of her brother-in-law beneath his condescending superiority. She worried for her sister living a life empty of all that she herself found so fulfilling. She remembered how as a child Emma had always been writing diaries and stories and had told Amy she wanted to be a writer when she grew up. Somehow now Amy could not connect with her sibling, who appeared to have a layer of superficial luxury between herself and reality. If they went out together, Emma would happily spend on a lunch what Amy could live on for a month back in Crete.

Amy took a last look out from her terrace as the lights were beginning to come on in Elounda. She went inside and locked the door and closed the shutters on the windows of her studio. Going downstairs she picked up her cabin bag and, with a feeling of regret she always felt on leaving her home, closed the front door and headed to the road where a taxi was waiting to take her to Heraklion.

She had easily managed to get a flight to London. The late-night plane was half empty but wearing a mask she found sleeping difficult. On landing she felt exhausted through lack of sleep and apprehension at seeing Emma. On the early-morning train from Gatwick to London she tried to drag her tired mind into the state of composure she knew she would need to support her sister. She bought a coffee on the platform at Clapham Junction before boarding the train to Esher where on arrival she was fortunate to find a taxi to take her to Emma's house.

The masked driver steered into the gravel drive and Amy paid. As she got out of the car Emma was at the front door. Amy had always considered her sister to be beautiful but the woman who awaited her looked dreadful. Emma's face was drawn, her piercing blue eyes bloodshot and her high cheekbones saddled with grey bags. Her long blonde hair was tangled and her slim figure shrouded in a hastily pulled-on gown.

Amy dropped her bag and ran towards her little sister, swaddling her in a hug. For minutes they stood there outside the house as Emma sobbed on Amy's shoulder. Emma was too distraught to talk and it took some time before the tears stopped enough for Amy to lead her inside, sit her down in the living room and head for the kitchen to make tea. The house was just as she remembered it: everything looking as though it was brand new, unwelcoming in its sterility. Almost afraid to move it, Amy filled the kettle and plugged it in, pulling open cupboard doors to find two mugs and some teabags. How unlike her own home this was.

While she waited for the water to boil she stared out of the glass folding doors which opened onto a patio then an immaculately manicured lawn, no doubt the work of a gardening contractor. She watched as a squirrel ran up the trunk of the impressive oak tree which formed a centrepiece for the lawn. A pair of magpies pecked at the grass looking for food.

The kettle clicked off and Amy poured water into the cups and got milk from the American-style fridge. The tea brewed, she returned to the living room. Her heart went out to the fragile figure on the edge of the large, cream leather sofa, her arms folded across her chest, her faced streaked in tears.

'Where's Nigel?' Surely Emma's husband must be around somewhere to look after his grieving wife, Amy thought as she asked the question.

'It's over. I've left him.' Emma just got the words out before she broke down again in sobs and Amy put down the mugs on the immaculately polished table and sat beside her sister, putting an arm around her and letting her cry.

She had always disliked Nigel but had kept her thoughts to herself for the sake of her sister. He had appeared to make her happy when they had married. She revelled in the comfort and security his high salary afforded them and he loved having a beautiful wife to show off at business dinners or to play host in their opulent home. Now it seemed the marriage had hit the buffers and deep down, Amy could not feel either surprise or regret at what had happened.

It took almost half an hour before Amy could make sense of what had happened. As Emma began to spill out the details of the breakup, it further confirmed to Amy that her instincts had been right and that her sister could only be better off without her smug, controlling husband. In disbelief she listened as her sister told her of the events of the previous days which had brought Emma's life crashing down.

Less than forty-eight hours earlier, Emma had driven down to see her mother in the Sussex countryside. She enjoyed these trips which had now resumed since a relaxation in the regulations. They were one of the few excuses she had to overcome her fear of venturing outside. Nigel was away on one of his many business trips which somehow appeared never to have been curtailed by any restrictions. Emma had arranged to have dinner with her mum and stay overnight before a day's shopping in Chichester. Usually her mother was on the doorstep to greet her. Emma got no response when she rang the doorbell and using her spare key went inside and discovered her mother's body.

Left alone after the paramedics had gone, Emma phoned her husband. In recent years this was something she had tried to avoid doing, as it seemed he was always busy at business functions and impatient to get her off the line. That evening was no different, Nigel's voice abrupt as he answered the phone. Before Emma could get her words out, she heard the unmistakable voice of a woman saying, 'Darling, shall I get us a glass of wine?'

At first Nigel had defensively claimed that he was working with his assistant. His response to the news of his wife's mother's death had not been to rush home to console her but to say he was very busy with work and would not be home for several days. For the first time in their marriage, Emma had exploded. The realisation of how little her husband cared for her and the likelihood that he was having an affair hit her. At the very moment she was at her lowest ebb, she found the strength to do what she should have done years ago and tell her husband that their marriage was over.

Suddenly she saw the years of their relationship for what they truly were. How she had been used and controlled by a man who would not even come to her side at the time of her greatest need. After she had hung up on his pathetic excuses and claims that she was being hysterical, Emma felt a mix of anger, fear and liberation all at once.

As Amy listened, she could feel her body tense with outrage at the way her sister had been treated. Emma's outpouring of anguish at her mother's death and her crumbling marriage were punctuated by cups of tea and coffee and it was late morning by the time she had calmed down enough to accept Amy's offer to cook them some breakfast. Amy tried to lighten the mood by telling her sister that lately being a shoulder to cry on had become her role in life. She persuaded Emma to go and have a shower and get dressed while she made toast, poached eggs, bacon and grilled tomatoes.

In the bathroom, Emma dared to confront her face in the mirror. Tears and tiredness had taken their toll. At her lowest ebb, she had always known that she was beautiful and what ate away at her was that this was her only worth. She envied the freedom her sister had grasped in leaving for Crete to be an artist. She had always harboured a sense of resentment that she had been left at home to be cosseted by her mother, who she had not been strong enough to stand up to.

Now her mother was dead, and her marriage was in tatters. The sister she so revered was downstairs cooking breakfast, but soon she too would be gone, back to her life in Greece. What had happened to her ambitions? Did she even have any? Through the fog of her memories, she struggled to catch sight of a past life beyond that of trying to please her mother and then her husband.

When their parents' marriage had ended, Emma had been denied nothing but the freedom to live her own life. She thought of her own daughter, Alice, already at university. Alice was a talented musician but had eventually succumbed to the arguments from her father that music was not a proper job and she should pursue the security of a business qualification. Emma had gone along with him, and Alice was now following a career path similar to that of her cheating father.

Emma turned the shower up as hot as she could stand. She scrubbed at her face, and sponged her body, then stood letting the hot water wash over her, watching the suds spiral down the drain. She towelled herself and dressed before drying and brushing her hair and applying some make up. Looking in her dressing table mirror, she caught the hint of a smile. 'You'll do,' she whispered.

When Emma came back down stairs, Amy was amazed to see her sister looking more like her old self but knew that the transformation was only skin deep. Amy spent the rest of the day weaving a course between Emma's fragile emotions and the practicalities of registering their mother's death, speaking to undertakers and solicitors. By the evening she was exhausted both emotionally and physically and her sister's brittle composure was beginning to flake.

'Shall we call it a day? I'm knackered.' Without asking, Amy went to the fridge, took out a bottle from the sizeable wine collection and returned to the sitting room with two glasses. 'I think we deserve this.' She poured the wine and pulled her mobile phone from her bag. 'What's it to be, Indian, Chinese, Thai, or something else? We'll get a home delivery.'

Whilst they awaited their Indian meal, Amy suggested they should go to their mother's house the following day to begin putting her affairs in order. Emma was exhausted and her mind was going everywhere but she was willing to do whatever her sister suggested.

*

Emma steered her Mercedes convertible with an assurance which came from familiarity with the route, even though it was pouring with rain. Behind the wheel she stared through the wipers going at double speed as they made their way along the country lanes to their mother's house. Amy thought about the last time she had seen her mother two years earlier. Like the other times she had visited, mother and daughter had failed to connect and Amy felt, as she always did, that their relationship was unfinished business. As they approached their mum's house, the realisation that for the first time she would not be there hit both women and they fell silent with their thoughts.

Pushing open the front door, Amy felt regret that she had not spent more time with her mother. For Emma it brought back the more recent memory of finding her mum's body. She took a deep breath, drawing in strength to contain her emotions. As Amy blinked away a tear, she looked across at her sister, giving her a reassuring smile.

'You make the coffee and I'll get started.'

Emma dutifully went to the kitchen, whilst Amy had a preliminary look around. Just as it had always been, the house was uncomfortably tidy. A few cookery books carefully lined up on a purpose-built shelf in the kitchen were the only sign of paper on the ground floor. Upstairs, Amy opened the door to her mother's room: the bed neatly made, cushions resting artfully on the pillows, the dressing table arranged with a few cosmetics, and no dirty washing in sight. A tear came to her eye as she caught sight of a framed photograph on the bedside table. Picking it up her mother and father looked back at her, their arms around a teenage girl and a child who Amy recognised as her younger self and her sister.

They were standing on grass against a background of a creek filled with moored boats of all shapes and sizes. From somewhere in her memory Amy recalled a day out the family had spent in Bosham on the coast in Chichester Harbour not far from their home. For some reason she remembered clearly her father telling her that King Canute's daughter was buried in the church outside of which the green was where the photograph had been taken. Wiping her eyes she turned and left the room.

She opened the doors on the other four bedrooms, every one of them cleaned and dusted to within an inch of its life. How unlike her own life had been her mother's, Amy thought, resisting the urge to pity her mother for the seeming sterility of the existence she had just left behind. She chided herself for making judgement and her thoughts settled on how little she had known her mother and, now that she had gone, how much she would miss her.

The one room left was what had at one time been her father's study. When she was a child she had not been allowed to play in there, although she remembered often seeing her father through the open doorway sitting in a chair, reading. She turned the handle and slowly opened the door, half expecting to smell the aroma of her father's cigarette smoke, but as she stepped inside there was no trace of the man who had deserted her mother all those years ago. Like the other rooms, this one was immaculately clean and tidy, as though its soul had been sucked from it with a powerful vacuum cleaner. Amy's disappointment turned to gratitude as she spotted what she had been looking for. In a row of clearly labelled files on the bookshelves lining the room it appeared was everything they had been asked to find by the solicitor. Taking the files from the shelves and looking inside, her hopes were confirmed. Her mother had been meticulous in keeping her affairs in order. Amy scooped up the files and took them downstairs, confident she could take them back to Emma's and locate everything that was required.

Emma was quietly grateful that her sister had already found what was needed. Neither of them was keen to remain any longer than necessary in the house and, after drinking their coffee, they washed up the mugs and closed the door on their past lives. Both women were relieved to have left the house. On the journey back the mood was lighter and Emma was keen to know how long her sister intended to stay. Amy was already missing her home in the village but reassured her sister that she would not be returning until their mother's affairs had been sorted out.

Back at Emma's house Amy called Andrew. She was relieved to hear him sounding happy as he chatted about working in the garden. He told her about how he had had to chase off a pair of goats which had escaped from a neighbour's smallholding, jumped the low wall and were just about to start dining on the plants.

Hanging up, she felt the pull of her adopted homeland deep inside but knew that for the time being her duty lay here with her sister.

They still had the stressful wait for the results of a post mortem. This was followed by weeks waiting for a slot at the crematorium for the funeral. With few people allowed to attend because of ongoing restrictions, the arrangements would be straightforward but the wait to have some closure seemed endless. The time was taken up putting their mother's affairs in order and with interminable hours drinking cups of tea.

As the weeks went by, the two women talked to each other more than they had since Amy left for art school and their parents' marriage had dissolved. Until that point the sisters had been close, Amy looking out for her young sibling and Emma in awe of the talented woman her sister had become. Since then they had grown further and further apart, the years and life having driven a wedge between them.

Both women hoped that this time together would bring them closer but, although the bond between them was strong, the legacy of the intervening years became more and more apparent. Deep down Emma resented her sister for leaving her to deal with the fallout from the collapse of their parents' relationship. She knew she had been spoiled by a mother desperate not to be deserted by the only family she had left; and sometimes she would catch an unwelcome glimpse of the snob she had been moulded into. She also regretted that she had not stood up to her husband as he discouraged their daughter from following her dream, and now feared that Alice was lost to her too. In those moments she hated herself but found she could not muster the strength to find a new direction.

Amy reflected on how she had left her sister to cope and felt guilty that she might have been partly responsible for what had happened since, the joy that had been sucked out of Emma in the pursuit of a lifestyle and security which had proved so stifling and had left her full of fear. On the outside there was no doubt she was a striking woman and the divorce and inheritance from their mother would leave her comfortable for life, but was it too late for her to take a different course? Amy discovered that her sister had no friends. Although the calendar on the kitchen wall was marked with events, it appeared they were all related to her husband's work.

*

Amy wiped away a tear as her mother's coffin disappeared through the curtains. She reached out and squeezed the hand of her sister who was desperately trying to retain composure. Apart from the vicar and the undertakers waiting outside, they were the only two mourners. Despite an easing of restrictions, Alice had made an excuse of the pandemic for her absence. The piped music of an organ played and Amy steered her sobbing sister out of the crematorium.

While Amy was relieved that her mother had been laid to rest, it would have been naïve of her to believe that Emma's sorrow would be buried along with her. As the days following the funeral wore on, Emma became more disconsolate and Amy longed to get home to her village on Crete but she could not leave her sister alone with her heartache.

To Amy, it felt as though every day was the same. Emma was like a lost soul drifting through the large house. Occasionally the two sisters would go out for a meal. All the administration of their mother's will was left in the hands of the solicitor so they did not even have that to keep them occupied. More and more Amy felt she needed the liberation of expressing herself through the broad stokes of her palette knife on canvas. She was missing her friends in the village walking society and the sound and scents of sea and mountains. She tried to sketch, but struggled to find inspiration inside the four walls of Emma's perfect home. She tried to seek solace in drawing small still lifes in pencil but would invariably be interrupted by her sister looking over her shoulder.

If Amy was frustrated by the monotony, she realised that for Emma this tedium was all she had to look forward to unless she could find a way to unlock a different door to the future. At forty years old, Emma still had plenty of life left in front of her to enjoy, if only she could let go of the past. Amy knew she could not stay in England but felt unable to leave Emma alone.

An idea had been forming in the back of Amy's mind but each time it surfaced she had pushed it away, not willing to confront the changes it would bring to the life she was so happy with. The way forward was obvious but it would not be easy. Amy knew she must try and persuade her sister to go back to Crete with her. Amy was protective of her independence and knew that Emma would struggle to share a life devoid of the luxuries and perceived status she was used to, but the alternative was too bleak to contemplate. If Emma was left alone she would descend into a pit of despair, a prisoner in her own home.

'Why don't you come back with me to Crete for a bit?' Amy grasped the nettle as the two of them sat over dinner in the kitchen at Emma's house. 'The sun always makes things feel better.'

'Oh, I'm not sure I could at the moment. There are still lose ends to tie up with Mum's estate and with the divorce going through there is just so much going on.'

Amy knew they were excuses. She persevered. 'All the more reason to get away from it all. And the solicitor is dealing with all that, and you can use your phone and email in Crete, you know.'

At first Emma was hesitant, but she was running out of reasons not to go. In the end it was the tough love of Amy planning to leave with or without her that persuaded a reluctant Emma to agree to travel to Crete, if only for a week or two. If Amy was relieved that she was going home, she calmed any slight anxieties she had about her sister coming with her by throwing herself into booking flights and doing the paperwork required to make the journey. Emma allowed herself to be organised. She packed her case and phoned Alice, who showed little interest that her mother was going.

Even in the taxi to the airport Emma complained about the early morning start and when she got there she moaned about the long wait to check they had the paperwork required. Not until they were on the plane was Amy sure that Emma would actually make the journey. By the time they were seated on the aircraft and Emma was still grumbling about the lack of legroom, Amy wondered whether she had been right to persuade her sister to accompany her home. Fortunately, the early start took its toll, and as Amy read her book, Emma fell into a deep sleep.

In her dreams Emma was in a dark place, alone and frightened, but as she awoke and saw Amy she remembered where she was. She was still scared of what the future held but she had her sister beside her. Turning her head the other way, she looked out of the cabin window. Thousands of metres below she could see the white wakes of tiny boats moving between islands which floated on the bluest of blue seas. As she craned her neck to get a better look, Emma felt the hint of a smile dance across her face.

The aircraft began its descent and Amy's expectations rose along with the discomfort in her ears. She swallowed hard and leaned forward to see out of the cabin window. Emma squeezed hard on her sister's hand as the mountains, their lower slopes swathed in olive trees, came into sight. Strips of golden sand and rocky coves girded the aquamarine sea and, as their plane levelled out for landing, they could see tiny figures on the beach below.

All of a sudden they touched down on the clifftop runway and were pinned back in their seats as the pilot engaged reverse thrust before turning the aircraft towards the terminal building. Amy thought how much better disembarking row by row from the aircraft was to the pre-covid scramble. When it was their turn, she led Emma forwards. As they stepped out into the blazing sunlight the heat hit them along with the smell of parched summer earth and herbs which blew in on the breeze from the mountains. She was home.

Coming Home

2021

TIRED AND TEMPTED by Emma's offer to pay for a taxi to the village, Amy nonetheless insisted they take the bus. She was determined that her sister's stay in Crete was not going to change the frugal lifestyle she cherished. Emma had already tutted at having to squeeze onto a bus to take them from the aeroplane to the terminal, then complained about the airport toilets and having to queue for the coach. It was early afternoon when they stepped onto the bus and found two seats near the back. The heat was stifling and wearing their facemasks made it uncomfortable, but as they set off and the air conditioning kicked in Emma had one less thing to complain about.

Although Emma appeared surprised by the relative luxury of the coach she was not enamoured as the driver began to speed his way along the national highway. She winced as he overtook slower vehicles with a blast of his horn. Her nerves rubbed raw by the wealth of new experiences, Emma was further irritated by her sister's seeming lack of sympathy to her concerns. Had she made the right decision to come to Crete? She leant her head against the bus window and fell asleep.

Although fatigued, Amy was too excited to sleep. She was relieved to be going home. The bus passed the outskirts of the party town of Malia and she smiled as it began to climb the gorge which carved a path towards the monastery of Agios Georgios, Selinari. She saw the driver take a hand from the wheel to cross himself as they passed the tiered tower rising through the trees, as she knew he would.

They were now getting closer to home as they sped through olive groves and orchards of almond trees surrounding clusters of white houses on the mountainside. Amy was tempted to wake her sister, but she was enjoying the moment of being alone with her thoughts and let Emma sleep on.

Amy finally had to wake her sister as they pulled into the bus station in Agios Nikolaos. Irritable at having been woken up and welcomed to town as they disembarked by graffiti-covered concrete walls, Emma complained when she learned they had to catch another bus to take them to Elounda. Amy resignedly wondered what her sister's reaction would be when she found out she would have to walk up the donkey track to the village when they got there! She was determined not to let Emma's mood spoil her homecoming, and led the way towards the Elounda bus, her sister mumbling in her wake.

Leaving behind the outskirts of the town the outlook changed. The road rose steeply above the Gulf of Mirabello. As they climbed higher, the scene became more spectacular. Emma was overwhelmed by it, but somewhere in her heart she felt sadness about the time she had lost to an unfulfilling past. The thought that she could not be happy even amidst such beauty scared her and sent her mind spiralling into anxiety. When they reached the crown, the loveliness was more than she could endure and she broke down in tears at her inability to experience the joy in the world.

Amy was shocked at her sister's reaction to the view which always uplifted her heart. Helping her off the bus on the quayside in Elounda, she enveloped Emma in a hug. Amy was now grateful for the walk they would have to take up the mountain to the village as she hoped it would distract Emma from the dark thoughts in her head.

Amy guided her sister across the square by the waterside to a taverna where the owner was a friend and agreed to take care of their cases until Amy returned for them later in her car. The pair then set off through the backstreets to where the donkey path began its way up the mountainside. Amy held her sister's hand tight as they climbed the steep incline. She was pleased to see Emma diverted from her innermost thoughts by the need to navigate the uneven cobbles and rocks which threatened to turn an ankle. They spoke little as they climbed, the silence between them accompanied by the incessant buzzing of cicadas and punctuated by the bleating of goats on the hillside pastures.

Thankfully, it was siesta time as they arrived in the village and the streets were deserted, so she managed to steer her sister to her house without drawing the attention of friends and neighbours to her homecoming. She smiled as she pushed open the front door but saw Emma grimace at the dark interior. As always Amy ran up the stairs, throwing open the shutters and windows and the door that opened onto the terrace, flooding the upstairs with sunlight before returning downstairs to open the shuttered windows on the ground floor.

Leading Emma up the staircase, she stepped onto the terrace and looked out on the familiar scene over the rooftops of the village houses and the olive groves to the iridescent bay below. Turning, she noticed a reluctant upturn in the corner of her sister's mouth as she took in what was laid out beneath her. Not saying a word, Amy crossed the terrace and pulled a chair up, then bade her sister to sit as she went indoors to fix them both a cold drink.

Amy got herself a chair and sat beside Emma. Taking a sip from her drink, she took in the panorama for which she had felt so homesick. Looking at her sister, Amy thought she could see an almost imperceptible softening of her features but it would take time before she would know if her decision to bring Emma to Crete with her had been wise.

Leaving her on the terrace, Amy walked over to the church of Zoodoho Pigi, beside which she had left her battered car. As she drove down the hillside to retrieve their baggage, she wondered whether she would be able to rescue Emma from the dark mood which had engulfed her. Had the tables been turned, would Amy easily be able to shrug off her past?

Parking by the quayside, she sat looking out across the row of brightly coloured caiques at their moorings. Had she been selfish to leave home when her sister had been just a child? She had always thought that she had stayed in Crete to live her best life and follow her career as an artist, but had she been running away from the disintegration of her family? She shook her head to dislodge the guilt that was building there and allowed her eyes to take in the waters of the bay and the bridge over the cutting which connected the mainland to the island of Kalydon. She determined to double her efforts to be patient with her sister and hope that giving her time and love would help her find happiness.

Amy hefted the cases into the house to find Emma was still in her seat, asleep again. One side of her face had reddened in the sun. Amy shook her awake. After moving their seats to the shade beneath the vine-draped pergola, Amy went inside and found a bottle of after-sun cream in the bathroom. Returning to the terrace she gently rubbed the lotion into her sister's face.

Standing, Emma walked back over to the wall surrounding the terrace and began to show signs for the first time of engaging with what she saw, asking questions of her sister. Amy found it hard not to feel pride and tried to restrain her enthusiasm in answering, worried that her passion might overwhelm the fragile stirrings of happiness that Emma was starting to reveal. She pointed out a rock on the ridge of the mountaintop which she thought looked like a giant goat and told the story of how the canal joining the bays of Korfos and Mirabello had been dug by French soldiers at the end of the nineteenth century. As Amy embarked on the story of the leper colony of Spinalonga, the small island just hidden from sight, she could see Emma still smiling but her eyes had begun to glaze over. Then the familiar bark of a dog interrupted her.

'Bella!' Amy called from the terrace. Looking down, Emma could see a black Labrador on the track below wagging its tail and barking up at them. Amy ran downstairs and bent to fuss the dog who responded enthusiastically by licking her face.

'I thought I heard voices.' Emma looked down from the terrace and along the track to where a tall, dark-haired man appeared.

'Andrew!' Amy rushed towards her neighbour and surprised herself by giving him a hug. It was only then that she realised just how much she had missed her friend. Something in him had changed, he seemed more relaxed and happier.

'Come down and meet Andrew,' Amy called to her sister.

As Emma left the house, Bella rushed up to her and licked her hand. She looked at her hand for a moment before wiping it on her dress and offering it to Andrew.

'This is my sister Emma.' Amy introduced her. 'It's so good to meet you, Emma.' Andrew stepped forward and took her hand. 'I think she likes you,' he continued and laughed, looking down at his dog.

Up close Emma could see the man was about her own age, maybe a year or two older; a few streaks of grey ran through his dark hair and the lines around his brown eyes smiled as he held her hand.

'It's good to see you home.' Andrew let Emma's hand drop and turned to Amy. 'You must be tired and hungry, so I wondered if you would like to join me for some food to save you the trouble of making something.'

Looking towards her sister, Amy saw her smile her agreement. 'We'd love to, Andrew. Can you give us an hour to get ready?'

'Come when you want. It'll just be salad, cheese, bread and some souvlaki on the barbecue. See you later.' Andrew called Bella and returned up the path in the direction of his house.

Amy let Emma use the bathroom first, showing her how to use the shower and taking the opportunity to explain the other quirks of the plumbing system, which were predictably greeted with distain by her sister. But when Amy emerged from her shower she smiled to see her younger sibling meticulously doing her make-up. Amy had not seen her sister taking so much care of her appearance since she had gone home to England after their mother died. She pulled on a pair on clean, un-ironed jeans and a t-shirt from her chest of drawers, quickly brushed her hair and tied it back in a bunch before slipping into a pair of flip flops.

'Am I overdressed?' Emma asked.

Amy looked at her sister, her hair shiny, make-up immaculate and wearing a white summer dress and matching white slip-on pumps.

'You've scrubbed up just fine. Let's go.' Amy grabbed a bottle of wine from the fridge and the sisters stepped out into the late-afternoon sunlight. The short walk allowed her enough time to explain to Emma about the death of Isabelle.

When the two women reached the gate in the wall surrounding Andrew's house, Amy could hardly believe the difference in the garden. If it had been splendid before, now it was stunning. In the months that she had been in England, the shrubs and trees that surrounded the terrace had flourished. Some of the more mature trees were even bearing fruit. Figs hung invitingly from branches and small unripe green olives flecked the silver leaves of their mother trees. The containers were ablaze with colour.

'It's amazing', said Amy as Andrew met them at the gate. She could see from the glow on his face the pride he took in the garden they had made together.

'And the view remains the same.' Andrew gestured towards the sweep of the mountainside tumbling towards the sea. Amy looked at her sister, her eyes moist as she stared down the hillside.

'I thought we could eat on the old terrace as the barbecue's there and it's nearer the kitchen.' Andrew led the women along the path cut through the trees and shrubs, emerging on the hidden terrace. The display which greeted them was breathtaking. The deep purple bougainvillea had established itself on the house wall and Amy saw how Andrew had carefully trained the burgeoning plant around the window and the still-broken door. Everywhere she looked her eyes alighted on a feast of colour: lilac pelargoniums, cream and yellow jasmine, pink oleander and red and white geraniums. Although no grapes hung from the vine, the tendrils had made their way across the full length of the pergola.

'I can't believe how much it has grown in just one summer. It's beautiful, Andrew,' Amy said.

'I couldn't have done it without you. Can I get you both a drink?' Embarrassed by the praise, Andrew disappeared inside.

'I'll just see if he needs a hand.' Amy followed him into the house, wanting to see how he really was and to mention her sister's fragile state. In the gloomy interior, Amy could see that if the garden had flourished, inside the house little had changed.

'I don't seem to get round to doing anything.' Seeing Amy glancing around, Andrew felt the need to explain. 'I like to be outside in the garden but when I'm inside, fixing up the house seems like a daunting task and my thoughts can still sometimes close in on me.'

'You've worked wonders with the garden,' Amy said cheerfully, handing him the bottle of wine she was clutching. 'It'll take time until you can get everything sorted.'

Andrew took a plate of souvlaki from the fridge followed by a bowl of salad and a chilled bottle. 'If you take the wine and glasses, I'll get the rest.'

Andrew lit the barbecue and whilst they waited for the coals to be ready, they sipped wine as the sun slid towards the mountains. Amy was keen to know news of the village. Andrew admitted that although the island had opened up to tourists there was still a nervousness about mixing with people and he had only been out to walk Bella and to shop.

Andrew served up the souvlaki they helped themselves to the salads and bread on the table. Neither of the women had realised how hungry they were following their journey and tucked in with relish. Their plates empty and with darkness falling, Andrew suggested they move to the other terrace. As the two sisters took seats, Andrew lit the candles in the lanterns. For a moment they sat in silence looking at Elounda below, at the lights in the houses and on the fishing boats scattered around the bay.

Amy thought how pleased she was to be home and hoped that being here would help heal her sister's scars. For herself, she desperately wanted to get back to work; she had so many ideas waiting to find expression on canvas. She decided that the following day she would try to return to a schedule of painting. Emma would have to entertain herself. Perhaps having to stand on her own two feet would be good for her. Turning, she realised her sister and Andrew were having a conversation. Looking up at the stars, she felt the reassurance of being in her allotted space in the universe, the place where she was meant to be. Somehow it assuaged any guilt she might be feeling about leaving Emma to her own devices.

*

Amy awoke to the familiar sounds of a cockerel crowing and the bleating of goats on the mountainside. For the first time since her mother's death, she felt lightness in her mood. She lay in bed, giving herself a moment to fully come round and embraced the contentment that being home at last had restored. Slithers of early-morning sunshine squeezed through cracks in the shutters. Despite the previous day's journey and a late night at Andrew's house, she felt refreshed and eager to begin painting. She opened the shutters and light flooded the room, bathing it in all the potential the new day had to offer.

She crept out of the room and silently opened the door to the bedroom where her sister was still sleeping before closing it and going to the kitchen. Taking a long-handled briki from the cupboard she measured a cup of cold water, a spoon of coffee and another of sugar into it and stirred before putting it on the gas ring and stirring again. She watched until the coffee began to foam and lifted the briki from the heat, returning it to the flame before the ritual was complete. After allowing the coffee to rest, she took a sip, filled a glass with water from the tap and went upstairs to the terrace.

In the early morning sun she sat and sketched out some ideas. The experience of putting her thoughts onto paper and the prospect of interpreting them through strokes of her brushes and palette knives filled her with excitement.

'Have you got any coffee?' Emma came onto the balcony in her pyjamas.

'Only Greek, I'll show you how to make it.' Amy led her sister back inside and down to the kitchen, instructing her on how to make a coffee in the briki. As she expected, her sister turned her nose up at the first sip but said nothing, which was a better reaction than Amy had anticipated.

'What shall we do today?' Emma enquired when they were back outside on the terrace.

'I'm going to work.' Amy gestured towards her sketchbook on the table. 'Why don't you take a look around the village, get your bearings. You could always walk down the donkey track to

Elounda.' Emma made a face as she remembered the walk up the hill the previous day. 'I may just have a quiet day, maybe a stroll around the village. I think I'll take a shower first.'

By the time Emma re-emerged, Amy had set up her easel and begun to paint. She thought how her sister looked rather overdressed for a walk through the village streets in the heat of the day.

'I'll give you a spare key, the front door is usually open but I need to go down to Elounda sometime to get us some food. So just in case I'm out.' Amy took a key off her ring and handed it to her sister. 'Enjoy your day.'

Looking down from the terrace, Amy saw her sister leave the front door and stop, deciding which way to turn before heading left and into the alleyways which wove their way through the village. Poor girl, thought Amy, but I'm sure she will eventually find her way.

Emma walked downhill along a narrow street lined on either side by small houses. Some appeared occupied but others were in a state of disrepair, even dilapidation. She looked through the empty window frame of a house which had almost been reclaimed by nature. Flowers and weeds had taken root in the earth floor and grew around an old table and chair. Much of the roof had fallen in and what was left of the beams was now exposed to the blazing sun. She heard a meow and looking for the source of the noise spotted a cat nursing its litter of tiny kittens in the shade of the table. The cat looked terribly thin, and Emma felt sorry for the mother, but had nothing to give her, even if she had been brave enough to enter the tumbledown building.

Further down the hill she rounded a corner. Two elderly women dressed all in black sat on chairs outside what appeared to be a closed café. They smiled, nodded and said something she did not understand, so she nodded and smiled back as she continued. A bit further down, the narrow lane turned into the donkey track she recognised from the day before, disappearing under a road which crossed above it. She had no intention of walking down the mountain track, particularly in her strapped wedge sandals, so climbed up to the road and headed up the hill.

When she could, she turned into a narrow street which led back into the village. She found herself in the dusty, walled courtyard of a small, stone chapel, perched on the mountainside. She stopped for a moment to get her bearings. Looking down on the bay reminded her of the previous evening at Andrew's house. She sat for a moment to rest on the wall. All this was so different to her. She thought of life back in England and was pleased she had decided to come to Crete. She thought of her mother and felt lonely. She thought of her daughter following in Nigel's footsteps and felt despair. She looked out again across the water to the scrubby hillsides of the island beyond and felt scared.

She stood up quickly to shake her thoughts and headed back into the streets. She would have liked a drink of water, but there were no shops. She continued exploring the winding alleyways, the silence accompanying her interrupted only by the buzzing of cicadas.

'Are you lost?' Emma was jolted from her reverie by a voice she recognised. She suddenly realised she was standing beside the gate to Andrew's house, on the other side of which was the man she had met the previous evening, standing watering his garden with a hose. 'Would you like a drink?'

'I'd love a glass of water if you don't mind.'

Andrew held the gate open for Emma, and led the way along the path to the house. 'Take a seat and I'll bring it for you.'

Emma watched as Andrew went through the broken door into the peeling house. What a contrast there was between the fabulous garden and the neglected interior. She could not understand how anyone could live in a state of such disorder. In her world, her home had always been tastefully furnished and decorated. The cleaner dusted and polished it to within an inch of its life.

'When are you going to start fixing up the house?' Emma asked before she could stop herself as soon as Andrew walked outside with two glasses of water. 'I'm sorry, that was awfully rude of me.' She tried to retrieve the situation.

Andrew put the glasses on the table.

'It's a fair question I suppose, and I'd like to say I haven't had the time to make a start yet. But of course, that would not be true.' He sat down. 'Without your sister I couldn't even have done this. She was the one who encouraged me to finish the garden my girlfriend Isabelle had always wanted. Somehow doing that kept her spirit alive and Amy helped me all the way.' Looking down at the stones on the terrace floor he continued. 'Although all this has helped me to grieve, I don't seem to be able to muster the energy to work on the house. Or to start on the book I had intended to write.'

'I wanted to be a writer once.' Where had that come from? Emma could not even remember when she had last thought of her ambition to become an author. It had long since been buried under the demands of her marriage and motherhood. 'Not like you, of course. It was only a childhood dream.' 'You should follow your dreams,' said Andrew. Then he raised his eyebrows. 'Listen to me! Who am I to talk?'

'But you've already achieved so much. Amy has told me about your work as a journalist. I've done nothing with my life.'

'I'm sure that's not true.' Andrew laid a hand on Emma's arm as he saw a tear come to her eye. 'Have you any plans for lunch? If not, I think I could rustle up something.'

'I'd like that.' Emma smiled.

Andrew got up.

'Let me help you,' said Emma, following him towards the door.

Inside, the house was dark, the shutters closed. Even in the meagre light which found its way through the open door, Emma could see dust everywhere, cobwebs in the corners and paint peeling from the walls. Andrew reached for a switch on the wall and turned on a dim bare light bulb which hung over the kitchen table. From the fridge he took tomatoes, cucumber, an onion, a chunk of feta cheese and a pot of olives. On the worktop was a loaf of bread which he handed to Emma along with a knife.

'If you don't mind slicing that, I'll make us a salad. I hope that will be OK?' Andrew asked.

'Looks perfect.' Emma picked up a board and began slicing. 'Can I do anything else?'

Andrew enlisted her help washing the vegetables as he made a Greek salad before taking a bottle of water and another of wine from the fridge and returning to the terrace.

As they lingered over lunch, the wine helped the pair open up about their past lives. Both realised that the other was lost; Andrew in his grief for Isabelle and Emma in her mother's death and the life she thought had been wasted, partly thanks to her marriage. As Bella sat in the shade beneath the table, the two damaged souls grew more and more at ease with each other about what had plunged their lives into such a dark place and, as they spoke, somehow that dark grew lighter.

'I really can't offer you anything but encouragement about writing your book. But I do know a bit about tidying up houses. Perhaps sadly, I rather enjoy it. Why don't I give you a hand?' Emma offered. 'If you can do the structural stuff, I can clean and decorate.'

Andrew thought about how, since he had become friends with Amy, she had often spoken about her sister. Although she had been disparaging about the lifestyle Emma had chosen, he could always detect affection in her words. Still, Emma had sounded to him like a person he might not like. On meeting her, much to his surprise, Andrew felt at ease in the company of this woman who in many ways was so different from himself. He didn't know what it was that he liked about her, but realised that in the short space of time he had known Emma, some of the weight of his depression had lifted.

He took the plunge. 'That would be great, if you have time?'

'Amy wants to get on with her painting so I'm at a bit of a loose end. You would be doing me a favour. How about we make a start tomorrow?'

'Why not? In fact, why don't we pop down to Elounda now and pick up some cleaning stuff, and some filler and sandpaper from the hardware store. We can go down the donkey track.' Andrew looked down at Emma's shoes. Or we can walk down the road.'

'I've not really adjusted to this new lifestyle, have I?' laughed Emma. 'If you don't mind walking slowly I'll be alright on the road.'

Andrew went inside to get his wallet and a rope lead for Bella before they set out on the road that weaved its way down the mountainside. It was late in the afternoon but the sun was still hot and Emma could feel drops of perspiration running down her back as she walked. On either side of them were olive groves dotted with smallholdings, their gardens bursting with vegetables and chickens running loose on the sun-baked earth. At every corner they turned the bay grew closer. But they hardly noticed their surroundings, both engrossed in conversation, making plans for the renovation of the house. By the time they reached the hardware store the list of shopping had grown to include tools, wood, paint, rollers and brushes.

'We'll never carry this lot back up the hill.' Andrew eyed the purchases they had amassed on the shop counter.

On overhearing this, the owner of the shop offered to deliver the supplies after he closed that evening. Andrew said he much appreciated it, and they left the shop feeling satisfied that a start had been made on the new project.

'As we're down here, would you like to go for a drink?' Andrew asked Emma.

Emma readily agreed, and they walked down the narrow street, emerging at a church beside the square on the harbour front. They followed the road that ran alongside the bay. Andrew pointed out the island of Spinalonga in the distance, boats making their way to it across the sparkling waters. Leaving the village behind, they arrived at a taverna beside a small beach. To one side of it they could see the frame of a boat under construction, and at the end of a stone quay was moored a caique.

'Welcome to The Boatyard.' A friendly woman speaking faultless English gestured for them to sit on the terrace. 'What can I get you to drink?'

As the woman went inside to get the beers they both ordered, Emma closed her eyes and let the warmth of the day wash over her before the silence was broken by the sound of glasses of ice-cold beer being placed on the table.

'Cheers,' said Andrew. 'And thanks for today. Without you I might never have got round to even thinking about fixing my place up.'

'I'm looking forward to it.' For a moment, Emma closed her eyes again, and in those few seconds realised that, for the first time in years, she might be happy.

A New Beginning

2021

AMY MARKED OUT her composition on the large canvas, using her sketches as reference. She then blocked in much of the background colour. She was pleased with her progress. Her enforced abstinence from doing the thing she loved best had given her a rush of creative energy and her head was bursting with ideas. It was late afternoon by the time she looked at her watch and realised her sister had been out for some time. The thought that she had perhaps walked down to the coast cheered her. Conceivably Emma was settling in to island life.

There was little more she could do to her picture until the paint had dried and she could begin working in some detail. She stood back and took a critical look at the canvas, making a mental note of things she wanted to over-paint. She took the canvas from the easel and moved it inside the house. All of a sudden a feeling of weariness came over her. Maybe she had grown unused to the heat since being away, or had the release of pent-up creative energy taken its toll? She sat down in the shade of the pergola and drifted off to sleep.

The light was changing towards sunset when she was woken by the sound of laughter and a man's voice which she recognised as Andrew's. Crossing the terrace, she looked over the wall to see her neighbour and sister walking up the lane towards the house. They were too engaged in conversation to notice her peering down, but Amy felt a warm feeling inside at hearing her sister's giggle for the first time since she was a child. Not wanting to break the spell, she just stood and watched. Seeing her sister happy confirmed in her mind that it had been the right decision to bring her to Crete.

They were almost outside the front door by the time they looked up and saw Amy.

'There you are. I was just having a sneaky sleep. Would you like to come in for a drink?'

'I'd love to, Amy, but I need to get home,' replied Andrew. 'The man from the hardware store is dropping off the stuff we need to get started on fixing up the house.' Amy raised an eyebrow and looked to her sister who gave a shrug and smiled. Perhaps bringing Emma to the island would have wider benefits; she had for some time been trying to persuade her neighbour to start work on his house, with no success. 'Thanks for the offer, and I'll see you soon.' Andrew called up to the terrace. Then he turned to Emma. 'And I'll see you tomorrow.'

'I'll be there,' Emma replied, opening the front door.

*

Keen to get working on her painting, Amy rose early the following morning. Something was not right. Light was filtering under her bedroom door. On opening it she saw the door to the terrace was open and the shutters on the windows had been thrown back. Sitting on the terrace was Emma, dressed in jeans and a t-shirt and drinking a cup of coffee.

'I hope I didn't wake you. I wanted to get off early to Andrew's so we can make a start on the house but I haven't really any suitable shoes to work in. Could I borrow a pair until I can get some of my own?'

Amy went back inside and picked up some flip flops from her bedroom floor before returning outside and handing them to her sister. 'You can have these if they fit. I've got several pairs.'

'They'll do fine,' said Emma, slipping them onto her feet and heading downstairs. 'I'll see you later.' Amy heard the door close and watched her sister walking up the lane and round the corner in the direction of her neighbour's house. As Emma disappeared out of sight, she felt a warm glow of wellbeing engulf her. Picking up her sister's cup from the table, she went inside to make herself a coffee to set her up to begin work.

Emma pushed open the gate and followed the path that wound through the fruit trees and shrubs. She was welcomed by the sound of sawing and Bella rushing up to her, barking and wagging her tail.

'I thought I'd make a start on this.' Andrew was kneeling on the door, which he had taken off its hinges and balanced between two chairs, and was trimming some wood off the bottom edge. 'If I can get it to fit, I think with some sanding and filling it should come up OK. Thank you for coming. Can I get you a coffee?' he offered.

'I've just had one, thanks,' replied Emma. 'Put me to work.'

'There's plenty to do. Make a start on whatever you want,' said Andrew.

Heading inside, Emma selected a bucket, a scrubbing brush and some clean cloths from the pile of purchases that had been delivered the previous evening. 'I'll begin the cleaning up and then we can see what we are faced with.' She shouted through the door, but doubted Andrew could hear over the sound of his sawing.

Opening the windows, she forced the shutters and let the fresh air and light flood the room before going upstairs and doing the same thing. Now she could see the task they faced it did not seem so daunting. She decided to dust away all the cobwebs first, then tackle sweeping the floors before washing all the surfaces. Then they could sand and fill the walls and ceilings before painting.

By the end of the day Andrew had repaired the front door and primed it in preparation for undercoating the following day. He would then be able to turn his attention to cutting out and repairing any rotten wood round the window frames and stripping the flaking paint from the shutters. Both Emma and Andrew were exhausted when they called a day on their hard work and sat having a drink on the terrace. Despite their tiredness, both felt a sense of elation at what they had already achieved.

'You two look knackered,' Amy said, appearing at the end of the path. 'I was wondering if you fancied eating in the taverna tonight? My treat. Alexander will think I've deserted him, we've been back three days already.' Amy laughed and stepped through the empty doorframe into the house. 'Wow! You two have been busy. It looks different already.' Amy came back out. 'Well, what do you think?'

'I'd love to. I haven't been in since it reopened,' replied Andrew.

'That sounds great. Count me in,' said Emma. 'But I must go home and freshen up first.'

Amy looked down at her paint smeared clothes. 'I think I could do with a change too. Why don't you call for us in half an hour, Andrew, and we'll be ready.' Amy looked at Emma who nodded her assent. They headed next door to get cleaned up.

Amy loved the simplicity of the local taverna, the bare, uneven flagstone floor, the rickety tables covered in paper tablecloths printed with a map of Crete, and the mismatched chairs. When they arrived, it was empty. Alexander stood up from where he sat behind the counter and beamed as they stepped through the door. Amy smiled back at the stocky, dark-haired owner as he walked towards them with open arms.

'My friends, I have missed you. Sit wherever you like.' Alexander gestured around at the tables and Amy introduced her sister to the taverna owner.

'We must drink a toast to your safe return.' Alexander went to the counter and brought back a carafe of raki and four glasses.

Pouring four measures, he slammed his glass on the table before downing the clear spirit in one. '*Yamas*, to our health!' Amy and Andrew followed suit, closely followed by Emma, who grimaced as the fiery spirit hit her throat.

'It's an acquired taste,' laughed Andrew. 'You'll get used to it.' He looked across the table at the two women who had come into his life. In each of them he could clearly discern the other. Both slim, blonde, blue-eyed and beautiful. In other ways how different they appeared, Amy self-contained and relaxed while Emma appeared to hold inside a pent-up energy. Amy swept aside her unruly long hair, and he noticed a fleck of blue paint on her tanned cheek. Emma's hair was cut short, framing a face perfectly made up to disguise a hint of sunburn. He pondered that, deep down, they were more similar than perhaps Amy realised.

Alexander appeared in no hurry to get their order and joined them drinking at the table. He told them how hard the lockdown had been for him, even since reopening, people were still reluctant to come out and hardly any tourists had ventured up the mountain from Elounda. Amy had just learned that none of her friends from the walking society had been in, when at that moment Stelios and Suzi walked through the door.

'You must have heard us.' Amy stood to greet her friends. 'We were just talking about you.'

Welcoming the couple, Alexander went to the bar to refill the carafe and get two more glasses as Amy pulled up more chairs. Taking off their facemasks the doctor and lawyer joined them at the table.

Seeing Suzi and Stelios, Amy realised how much she had missed them. Both short, dark-haired and smartly dressed they made a handsome couple who complemented each other perfectly. Although outwardly more serious than Amy, she valued their friendship, kindness and good counsel which over the years she had grown to value.

Eventually Alexander took their order and made his way to the kitchen to cook up plates of mezzes. Short sticks of pork souvlaki, spicy village sausages, horta omelette, small fried fish, cheese croquettes, salads and much more. Andrew and Stelios dragged up another table so they could find room for the plates of food which kept coming.

Amy explained how she and her sister had just got back from England after their mother's death. Stelios told of how he had gone to work in the hospital in Agios Nikolaos to help out in the pandemic whilst Suzi was struggling to keep her law practice afloat. Both Andrew and Emma were pleased to meet Amy's friends and conversation soon moved on to the walking society. Neither Stelios, Suzi or Amy had seen any of the other members in over a year. With the taverna having been closed and meetings of groups forbidden, the habit of their Friday night meetings had been broken. It was settled that they should try to get the group back together. At the very least Alexander could do with the custom, and now things were easing a bit some long treks in the countryside would do everyone good.

As the wine flowed, they reminisced about walks they had done in the past, and Andrew said he would like to join them on their next hike when it was arranged. Amy agreed that she would try to contact the other members of the group and see if they could meet up on the following Friday. In the meantime she would look for a route that would ease them back into walking again.

Alexander left the kitchen and took his lyra from the wall and joined them at the table. For Emma, it was the first time she had heard the haunting tones of the magical instrument and when Alexander drew his bow across the strings, she fell under its spell. As the musician warmed to his task, Stelios moved tables from the centre of the room and began to dance, slowly at first before picking up the pace as the music got faster. Gesturing to the others to join him, both Suzi and Amy took to the floor, linking arms around each other's shoulders.

It wasn't long before Emma and Andrew had been encouraged to leave their seats and join in, Amy showing them the steps. It surprised her how quickly Emma picked up the rhythm and Amy felt a wave of affection sweep over her as she watched her sister abandon herself to the music. Andrew was more reluctant to release his inhibitions but, encouraged by Emma's enthusiasm, he found himself immersed in the dance as Stelios led the line out of the taverna and into the street. Whether it was the raki, the wine or the music, Emma could not remember a time when she had felt freer. When the music stopped, she hurried back to her chair, unnerved by this new feeling of liberation. Amy was delighted that her sister had let go the reins of her emotions and encouraged her to re-join the dancing, but it was Andrew who persuaded her to get back on her feet.

Emma lost herself in the dancing. She did not notice her sister had returned to her chair. It was only after Stelios had left the floor and had sat down to talk with Amy that the spell was broken and, laughing, the others returned to the table. Nobody wanted the evening to end but Stelios had consultations early the next morning, Amy felt tired and Andrew was keen to maintain the momentum on fixing up his house the following day. Thanking Alexander they departed, Amy promising to try to get the walking group together the next week. Stelios and Suzi headed towards the donkey track as the others began to make their way up the hill towards their homes.

Stelios turned. 'Hope to see you next Friday, and remember Amy, pop in and see me before then.'

Andrew raised an eyebrow at his friend.

'He's got some ideas for walks. He did suggest a trek up Mount Ida but it's getting too late in the year, and I think it's a bit ambitious for some of us until we get some practice in,' Amy said.

Ever since the day Nick had told her of the tallest mountain on the island all those years ago, Amy had dreamed of climbing it. At the thought of her ex-lover, she felt a moment of regret but the prospect that they might attempt the trek filled her with excitement.

'Isn't that the tallest mountain on Crete? I wouldn't mind giving that a go.' Something in Andrew felt inspired by the challenge.

'Maybe next year,' said Amy, 'It will take a bit of organising and we'll need to make sure the weather is good. We'll have to wait until the winter snows have melted on the upper slopes and I believe the best time to do the climb is overnight before it gets too hot. It's something to think about, and some of the group might take some persuading, but in the meantime I'll try and come up with a gentler route.'

*

Amy was as good as her word, and by the following Friday she had managed to get together all of the group, except for Emer and George, who Amy sensed were still reluctant to mix with people.

The others seemed keen to resume seeing their friends and to get some exercise. Over dinner at the taverna, they all agreed to tackle walking the gorge in the nearby village of Kritsa. Amy assured the group that there was a 'lazy' route, not too taxing, for those of them who felt nervous about taking on a challenging hike.

The trek was a success and a welcome liberation from the strictures of the last year. After the aches and pains of that first walk had been soaked away, the society met up as often as possible to take on more routes before autumn came to an end. Even Emer and George had eventually been persuaded to join them again and by the time the nets had been laid in the fields for the olive harvest, the group was complete again. Emma and Andrew were a welcome addition to the gang of walkers and became two of the most enthusiastic participants, usually stepping out at the front on their hikes through the mountains.

As autumn moved into winter, Andrew and Emma had made real progress on the house. Whenever Amy visited her neighbour, she was amazed at what she saw. Perhaps even more surprising to her was the determination of her sister to get the job done. She had never seen her so fulfilled and, since they had started the work, Emma had not missed a day helping Andrew out and showed no sign of wanting to return to England. Amy was happy at the thought that maybe there was more to Emma staying on in Crete than perhaps her sister herself realised. After they had cleaned and painted the walls of the house, other jobs began to reveal themselves. Emma learned from the internet alongside Andrew how to fit skirting boards, fix leaking taps and lay tiles. What had started out as an attempt to make the house habitable had expanded into making it a home.

At first, Emma had found the inevitable calls with her solicitors dragged her mood down but as Andrew's house began to take shape she found she was more able to cope with the difficulties of her impending divorce. Despite the dips in her mood that these phone calls precipitated, week by week these became less profound and Amy noticed her sister's increasing resilience, despite the one dark cloud which remained on the horizon.

Since the breakup of her marriage, relations between Emma and her daughter had been strained. They had kept in touch with the occasional phone call but since Emma's mother's death, the pandemic and Alice's studies at university had proved a convenient excuse for them not to meet. The last time they had spoken they had argued, Alice blaming her mother for the failure of her marriage and not fighting hard enough to keep the family together. Amy tried to reassure her sister that Alice just needed time to adjust to the situation but knew in her heart that beneath Emma's new-found confidence the soured relationship with her daughter played on her mind.

With Emma absorbed in working on Andrew's house, Amy was glad to be able to paint without interruption. She had been offered an exhibition in Agios Nikolaos and was working hard to complete some new pictures for the show. With the weather getting more unpredictable, the group took less challenging walks, often along the coastline or on paths with which they were more familiar.

As the year drew to its close, Andrew and Emma could finally see an end to their work on the house. In the first few days of December Andrew busied himself with the snagging, whilst Emma searched online for furnishings to make the house more homely. They were proud of what they had achieved and it was Andrew who suggested that the three of them should spend Christmas in his newly renovated home. At first Emma was unsure as she held out hope that she might visit Alice at Christmas, but when it became clear her daughter was spending the holiday with Nigel and his girlfriend she came round to the idea.

Emma was adamant that they celebrate Christmas in a traditional English way and took charge, volunteering to cook the Christmas dinner. She made a Christmas pudding and fed it with Metaxa for weeks before the day. She struggled to find a turkey in Elounda, so ordered a chicken from the butcher. As Christmas Day grew nearer, she took over the dressing of the house, making decorations and buying scented candles. She went to Agios Nikolaos and bought the best wines she could get and somehow found someone who would deliver them logs for the fire. She made her own stuffing for the bird with apple, breadcrumbs, sage, onion and sausage meat.

Amy was used to Christmas being a low-key affair but was delighted to see her sister so happy. The change she had seen in her since she had come to Crete several months earlier was more remarkable than she could have hoped for. Andrew too appeared more at ease. She could tell he still had his dark moods, but from what she could see, these were becoming less frequent. He seemed more tolerant of some of Emma's foibles than Amy. She noticed how he would just laugh off some of the things Emma said, while she would be irritated by them.

The big day dawned clear and bright, the late-rising sun taking the chill out of the air as they sat on the terrace and toasted Christmas. Inside Andrew's house, Emma had set a fire in the grate ready to light and had laid the table and decorated it with flowers and candles. She had crafted three Christmas crackers and opened a bottle of red wine to breathe. Emma was adamant that she needed no help from her sister, and Amy had to admit she was impressed with Emma's hosting skills. She had a list of when to put things in the oven, and set the timer on her phone to remind her of each stage.

Sitting in the winter sun, they exchanged gifts. Despite a mutual agreement not to spend more than 30 euros on each present, Amy was pleased but embarrassed to open a gift of a new pair of walking boots from her sister. She meanwhile had bought Emma a leather-bound notebook which she hoped would spur her on to pursue her ambitions to write. From Andrew, Amy received a new waterproof jacket. Emma had also broken the budget in her gift to Andrew when she presented him with a timed irrigation system for his garden. Emma was stunned when she unwrapped a necklace, a sapphire mounted in silver in the shape of an eye. She had seen the symbol painted on boats in the harbour but had not thought to discover its significance.

'It's to keep you safe,' Andrew whispered as he fastened it around her neck.

Disappearing down the path, Amy returned carrying a large package which she had left hidden behind a shrub. As Andrew unwrapped his present, he was amazed at the beautiful multi-canvas painting of his house through all the stages of its renovation, which had been completed with a picture of it now, surrounded by the beautiful garden he had created with Amy in memory of Isabelle. He was desperate to hang it there and then but it would require some substantial fixings to secure it so reluctantly he propped it against the wall, finding it difficult to stop glancing across at the bewitching framed canvas.

The sun drifting down towards the mountaintops heralded a chill in the air and they moved inside and lit the fire before sitting down to dinner. From the kitchen Emma brought plates of homemade paté, Melba toast and onion chutney.

'That looks wonderful, Emma. Would you like me to pour the wine?' Andrew asked, picking up the bottle from the table.

All seated and glasses charged, Andrew raised his drink in the air. 'Merry Christmas. And a toast to those we have lost. To your mum,' he looked across and saw tears in both the women's eyes. 'And to Isabelle. She would have loved all we have achieved. Thank you to both of you for helping me do it.'

'I'm sorry, that's my phone.' Emma leant down beside her and rummaged in her bag. 'It's Alice.' Swiping the screen, she spoke into her mobile. 'Happy Christmas, darling… I'm at a friend's house… Why? Where are you?' Amy and Andrew could see the shock on Emma's face. 'Further up the hill from Auntie Amy's. I'll come out to the road.' Emma stood up and made for the door. 'It's Alice. She's here.'

Emma made her way to the gate in the dry stone wall. Through the gathering darkness she recognised the solitary figure of her daughter trudging up the hill, pulling a small case on wheels.

'Alice!' Opening the gate, Emma rushed towards her daughter and hugged her. 'What on earth…?'

'It's a long story. Almost as long as the journey. Can I come in?'

Amy held her niece tight and kissed her. 'Hello Amy,' said Alice shyly.

'What a lovely surprise. This is Amy's neighbour Andrew.' Emma introduced Alice to their host.

Andrew could see that Alice was unmistakably her mother's daughter, but the grey shadows beneath her eyes and her unkempt hair told a story of more than what had obviously been a long journey.

A place was set for Alice at the table and she seemed relieved to be able to sit. Amy made her way to the kitchen counter. 'Pour Alice a drink and talk and I'll rustle up another starter.'

From across the room, Amy perceived the anguish in Alice's exhausted face.

Looking at her daughter, for the first time in years Emma could see vulnerability. Emma's heart went out to Alice. She saw now that her little girl had been a victim of her husband's controlling personality in the same way that she had. With this came the realisation that she had been the adult in the relationship, and she regretted that she had been unable to fight for her daughter's future. For the first time she was seeing the past through new eyes.

Whilst they ate, Alice explained how, from the first day she had arrived at the house her father now rented with his girlfriend to spend the Christmas holidays, she had sensed that her dad's new woman resented her presence. As the days went by, the bad atmosphere between them escalated and it became obvious that Alice would get little support from her father. The evening she had walked out, her father had done nothing to stop her, and she had not heard from him since.

Distraught and having nowhere to go, she thought of spending Christmas in Crete. Her confidence was shaken by her father's rejection and, frightened of being dissuaded from coming by her mother, she decided to surprise her. Unable to fly direct, she had managed to get a ticket to Athens and then transfer to the last internal flight on Christmas Eve. By the time she arrived at Heraklion it was late at night so there were no buses or taxis. She had spent the night in the airport, before hitchhiking to Agios Nikolaos. There were few cars on the road from the town to Elounda and it had taken her hours to get a lift there. She followed the map on her phone and took the track up the mountainside to the village. She had panicked when she found there was nobody in at Auntie Amy's house, and that's when she had rung her mother's phone.

Hearing Alice's story, Emma was furious at her husband's treatment of their daughter but had not felt such happiness for years as to have her by her side. In turn, Alice was relieved to have received such a loving welcome from her mother. There was plenty of food for all of them and when the meal was finished, Andrew suggested the women take their drinks outside while he did the clearing away and washing up.

The evening was clear and cold and Amy led the way through the trees to the front terrace. She lit the three lanterns that stood on the wall. Below, the lights of Elounda twinkled and, for once, not one boat ruffled the ink-black waters of the bay. Alice sat down and breathed in the view and the silence, and felt a surge of happiness wash over her. Tilting her head back, she looked up at the stars and drifted off to sleep.

'You must be exhausted. Let's get you back and make you up a bed.' Emma roused her sleeping daughter. 'You stay here,' she said to her sister. 'I'll see you back at home. Thanks for a wonderful day. Happy Christmas.' Putting one arm around her daughter, the other taking her case, she steered both towards the gate and disappeared down the lane.

Emma felt a rush of tenderness as she made up the sofa bed in Amy's studio. As she plumped up the pillows and smoothed out the sheets, she thought of how far she had come since the demise of her marriage. She had been almost broken by the betrayal of her husband and the death of her mum, but in this moment her heart almost burst with the joy of finding her daughter again. As Alice's head touched the cool pillow, Emma stroked her hair and by the time she whispered, 'Goodnight, darling,' she was asleep.

Alice awoke to the sound of voices talking quietly. The room was still in darkness and for a moment she was unsure where she was. As she came to, she remembered she was in Crete with her mother, and the Christmas dinner they had shared the night before. She got up and found her bag, and reached inside for her phone. She was surprised to see it was already ten o'clock. She walked towards the voices and opened the door to the terrace, flooding the room with light.

'I'm sorry, did we wake you? We crept through the room as quietly as we could. We thought you might need a lie-in. Can I get you a coffee?' asked her mother, crossing the terrace and giving her a hug.

'No thank you, if it's OK I'll have a shower first. Wow! That's sensational,' Alice said as she caught the view down the mountainside. Through the clear blue of the winter sky, the enamel sea glinted like a jewel. For a moment she just stared. Emma watched as a smile spread across her daughter's face. 'I must go and get myself ready, it would be a shame to waste any more of the day.' Alice turned and went back inside to the room where she had been sleeping. Opening the shutters, she could now see the studio. On the walls hung finished canvases which, up close, she saw had been signed by her aunt. Another large, unfinished painting rested on an easel in the corner and a number of other pictures lay resting against the walls. Alice was not an expert but she knew enough to realise these were serious works of art.

In the past when she was younger, her parents, in particular her father, had always been dismissive of her aunt's work as an artist, as though it was just something she did to while away the hours and not a proper job. Hadn't that been her father's attitude to her ambitions to become a musician? But even in the few hours she had been here, she had seen how content her aunt was. She owned this house with its amazing view and had created these striking paintings. Had her father's wealth bought him happiness? When she thought of her current career path a cloud passed through her head. Was that what she really wanted, to be rich like her father? Until recently, her mother had been caught up in the money obsessed world of her husband, and she had been miserable. Alice pushed the thoughts of her future aside. She could stay here for almost two weeks before she needed to return to university and was determined to embrace the wellbeing she had begun to feel. Even her mother seemed changed by the island.

By the time Alice had showered, dressed and drunk a coffee it was almost lunchtime. Emma suggested they all go for a walk down the mountainside to Elounda to see if they could find a taverna open that would serve them lunch.

'I think I'm going to stay and do a bit of work on my painting. Why don't the two of you go, you must have a lot of catching up to do.' Amy went into her studio and carried the easel and her unfinished painting out into the sunlight.

On the walk down the donkey track to the sea, Alice could sense her mother's enthusiasm as she talked about the village and the island. It was hard for her not to be infected by Emma's new-found delight. They found a taverna on a road just off the square which was open, and over a salad and glass of wine her mother told Alice of the friendships she had made, not just with Andrew but with members of the walking group. Momentarily a ripple of fear passed through Alice's mind. Ostracised from her father, she felt England might be a very lonely place with her mother so far away.

Seeing her daughter's face drop, Emma leaned across the table and took her hand.

'Why don't I come back to England with you after the holiday? You've only got a couple of terms left at university and we can make decisions about the future when you have got your degree.'

'No, you must stay here Mum. I'm just being selfish. You must do what's right for you. I've never seen you so happy. The time will fly, and Crete's not so far away.' A smile returned to Alice's face as she lifted her glass. 'Merry Christmas, Mum, and here's to a very happy new year.'

The sea was like a mirror, the sky crisp and clear as mother and daughter walked along the causeway towards the canal. They stood on the bridge and looked across the bay towards the leper island of Spinalonga. Beside the cutting stood two windmills, their sails long since dismantled, and the empty terrace of a taverna closed for the winter. Strolling back towards Elounda they looked up the mountainside and could see the village glistening white. The winter sun was low in the sky before they set off up the donkey track, so deep in conversation that neither woman noticed the steepness of the climb.

When finally they reached the house, went upstairs and stepped out onto the terrace, Emma laughed when she saw her sister dozing in a chair.

'Caught you! So that's what you call work?'

Amy rubbed her eyes and smiled. 'I think I've made some good progress.' She glanced over at the easel. 'But yesterday's late night must have taken it out of me a bit.'

'I love your picture.' Alice stared at the painting which was even more vibrant in the afternoon sunshine.

'When I finish it, it's yours. A Christmas present from me.'

For a moment Alice was speechless. Feeling the tears welling up, she bent down and embraced Amy.

'Thank you. Thank you.'

Alice stood up and nervously brushed her long blonde hair back behind an ear. How the tall, slim young woman reminded Amy of Emma when she was younger. In that moment she revealed a vulnerability and Amy knew that beneath the t-shirt, black leggings and trainers lay a slightly awkward young woman still uncertain of her place in the world.

'We might have to package it up and get it sent to you in the UK. I think it would be a bit bulky to take home with you on the plane,' said Amy.

Alice's face fell; the reminder that she would be returning home soon cast a shadow over her buoyant mood. She had been reunited with her mother and aunt for less than twenty-four hours but that day had been the best she could remember. She thought about what her mother had said earlier; that Crete was not far away. Anyway, it was not long until her graduation and then she could decide what she would do with her life. Those thoughts restored her equilibrium and when her aunt asked her and her mother if they would like to eat in the local taverna that night, she banished all negative emotions to the depths of her mind.

Amy had not seen the taverna so full since before the pandemic. Joined by Andrew, the four of them took the last table inside. Alexander was beaming at the rush of custom and had lit a fire in the grate to ward off the evening chill. It appeared that the entire walking group had shared the same idea about coming to the taverna and Alexander made a great show of moving the tables around so they could sit together. Jugs of red and white wine and bottles of water appeared and as the friends shouted out their preference of mezzes, Alexander scribbled them down on the paper tablecloth. When the food came the table was laden. Amy and Emma explained to Alice what each dish was and she found everything delicious.

The room was full of laughter and people shouting greetings of the season. Emma could not see how they could fit any more food on the tables. Then the door opened and a pretty, slim woman in her early forties, tanned, her shoulder-length hair bleached almost white by the sun entered carrying a guitar case. She appeared to know most of the customers and space was made for the musician at another table. Emma was excited when Amy explained to her that the guitarist was an Englishwoman called Phoebe who lived in the village and had had a recent hit in the UK with a song she recognised.

'Where's Andreas tonight?' Amy asked as Phoebe came over to wish her a happy Christmas. As the woman bent to hear Amy, Alice noticed the exquisite gold pendant of two bees which hung from her neck.

'At home with the kids. They were both exhausted after the excitement of yesterday.'

'I know the feeling,' laughed Amy. 'I didn't know you were playing tonight. What a lovely surprise.'

'I didn't either, but I bumped into Alexander today and he thought it would be fun.'

'It seems word's got out about the music.' Amy nodded towards the door. The tables outside were beginning to fill with customers muffled against the cold.

'I'm just going to grab something to eat before we start. I'll catch you later.' Phoebe returned to her table and the conversation turned to the following year and plans the friends had for more adventurous walks when the days grew longer and the weather warmer. As the drink flowed, the group's ideas grew more ambitious. In his enthusiasm Andrew suggested they take on the challenge of walking the length of the island, before realising the impracticality of his idea, particularly with most of the group having work commitments. But he held onto his thought; perhaps it was a challenge he could take on alone, or at least with Bella. In the end they agreed to walk some of the many gorges on the island, the Richtis Gorge to the east and the Imbros Gorge to the west.

'Why don't we try and climb Psiloritis, Mount Ida?' Amy suggested.

Like Amy, Andrew harboured an ambition to take on the challenge of Crete's tallest mountain and enthusiastically endorsed the suggestion. They would have plenty of time to prepare for an ascent in the late spring. The more they talked about the idea, the keener the group became. Once the Christmas holidays were over, Amy would try to find a guide and organise the expedition, spurred on by the prospect that her dream of climbing the mountain might at last come true.

Alice's eyes suddenly lit up at the sound of instruments being tuned where, in a far corner of the room, Phoebe had been joined by Alexander with his lyra. Sensing the music was going to start, the conversation grew quieter and Alice felt the tingle of excitement she always experienced when she was about to hear live music.

Alexander took the lead, drawing the bow slowly across the strings of his lyra. The sound seemed to penetrate every corner of the room and then into the dark of the night where it flew away into the mountains, and through the olive groves to the sea. Its long, ethereal notes burst into Alice's head, permeating her soul, before the more familiar sound of the guitar reined the melody into its rhythm.

The music was unlike anything Alice had ever heard. Somehow it stirred in her something she had thought had been long lost. She felt its power and the joy welling up inside her and as it built to a crescendo she hardly noticed the tears in her eyes. Entranced, she felt her mother's hand on her shoulder. Emma and Amy stood and urged her to join in as they linked arms around the shoulders of their friends, but she smiled and shook her head, watching contentedly as her mother and aunt danced out of the taverna into the street. Alice sat captivated as Alexander and Phoebe played. She looked through the window at the elated dancers, then looked into her soul and rediscovered a happiness she thought had gone forever.

On Psiloritis

2022

AMY SMILED AS she looked across the table at her sister speaking with Andrew and laughing. She had noticed that in recent months they had grown closer and felt reassured. She sat in silence, taking in the warm buzz of conversation at the long table which had been laid for them. There was a chill in the spring air on the high plateau where they had arranged to meet their guide for the long-planned hike to Timios Stavros, also known as Mount Ida, the tallest peak in the Psiloritis range and the highest point on the island.

Lost in her feelings, Amy drifted back to the hike through the Samaria Gorge nine years earlier. She was warmed by the thought that, apart from Nick, all the same friends had taken up this challenge. She had no regrets about her decision not to marry Nick and to stay on Crete. This was the place which made her the person she wanted to be, and she intended to live here for the rest of her life.

The friends had set out in a convoy of three cars from Elounda in the early afternoon. In the square on the waterfront the warm spring sun shone full of promise. The drive along the coast had been leisurely. West of Heraklion they turned inland, climbing steadily towards the foothills of the Psiloritis range. As they rose higher they could feel the temperature drop and the olive groves gave way to pastures scattered with wildflowers. Above, in the ice blue sky, Amy had spotted a golden eagle floating on the thermals over the mountains. How amazing it would be to soar up to the heavens, looking down on the island which had been her home for so many years. The sight of the bird fuelled her excitement for the climb ahead and what she might see from the pinnacle.

Arriving at the village of Anoyia, Amy remembered the stories of how it had been razed to the ground during the Second World

War. Its menfolk had been rounded up and massacred by the Germans in reprisal for the abduction of their commander General Kreipe in an undercover operation by Allied and resistance fighters in 1944. At the cafes on the square, men dressed in traditional baggy trousers tucked into long boots enjoyed a smoke and drank coffee or raki whilst swinging komboloi beads or playing tavli. Eagle-eyed widows in black mufti sat outside shops on the lookout for tourists to buy a woven rug or embroidered tablecloth.

Outside the village the road climbed again. Amy felt the pressure in her ears as they ascended. The few trees that grew here were stunted, and the sheep and goats grazed on the meagre pickings of dry grass and low prickly bushes. On the mountaintops she could see a scattering of snow gleaming white in the sunshine and on the lower slopes the tumbledown dry-stone walls of small shepherds' huts. Suddenly the road crested the slope, revealing the Nida Plateau beneath. It was late afternoon by the time they skirted the edge of the plain and found the taverna where Amy had arranged to meet their mountain guide.

Amy was tempted by a cold beer but, mindful of the overnight climb that lay ahead, settled for lemonade. True to his word their guide arrived in time to join them for an evening meal, and introduced himself as Nikos.

Before they ordered food, Nikos went through a checklist of things he had asked the hikers to pack, including warm clothing, torches, sleeping bags, high energy snacks and drinks, and confirmed they were wearing two pairs of socks. He told them that he would take the pace of the slowest of the climbers and they would have plenty of time to reach the peak of Timios Stavros before dawn, so there was no need to hurry. Safety was the most important thing but conditions were good, although there was still a thin covering of snow near the top.

Nikos advised them to eat well before they set out, and as the sun began its descent behind the mountains, the table began to fill up with plates of mouthwatering lamb kleftiko. Nikos told them how this dish had originated when groups of resistance fighters hiding in the mountains from the Ottoman occupiers had slowly cooked meat buried underground so the smoke would not give away their hideouts.

Wrapped in parcels of parchment, the dish had been slow-cooked in the oven with potatoes, goats' cheese, garlic, lemon, tomatoes and mountain herbs. Peeling open the paper, Amy could see the fragrant hot steam rising in the cool evening air. It warmed her face and the delicious smells whetted her appetite and gave her a sense of wellbeing. Looking around, she noticed her friends sitting at the table had gone silent as they set about eating their first mouthfuls of the dish.

The mountains were now shadows, black upon the darkness of the oncoming night. Above them stars shone brightly; Amy imagined them lighting the way to some distant galaxy. A shooting star pulled its trail of light across the heavens and Amy wondered how she could take such delight feeling so small in the midst of infinite vastness.

Coming back to earth she heard the voice of Nikos enthusiastically talking to Juliette and Mike about a massive sculpture called the Andarte of Peace which had been constructed from boulders on the plateau. Made from more than five thousand rocks, from above it represented a winged figure. It was the concept of a German sculptor, laid with the help of local people as an act of reconciliation for the atrocities committed by the occupying German army during the Second World War.

Going further back to ancient legend, Nikos recounted the tale of Zeus, who was said to have been brought to the nearby Idean Cave from his birthplace in Lassithi to escape his father Kronos, who was intent on murdering his son because an oracle had warned he would depose him. In the foothills of the mountains the young god was protected by the fearsome Kouretes warriors who would bang their spears on their shields to drown out the baby's cries and keep his presence secret. Kronos had been right to be afraid, as on reaching adulthood Zeus ganged up with his siblings and overthrew their father, drawing lots to divide the kingdoms of the world they had conquered.

As she listened, Amy's thoughts flitted to the timeless nature of her adopted homeland and she felt content to have been a tiny part of its inexhaustible history. When she tuned in again to the conversation, Nikos was explaining that the stone huts on the mountainside, called *mitata*, were shelters built by shepherds, where in the past they would sleep and make cheese, while now they were mostly used as shelters for their flocks and as chicken coops.

Above her on the mountain, Amy could make out lights and asked Nikos about them. He told her they were fires lit by climbers who had set off earlier. It was nearly midnight before they called for the bill and the friends ran through a final checklist with Nikos. He told them he would lead and asked Stelios and Suzi if they would bring up the rear and not let anyone fall behind. If anyone needed to stop for a rest, then it was essential that the whole group wait with them. He stressed again that they would reach the top long before dawn so there was no need to push the pace for fear of missing the sunrise. If things went well, they should even have time to catch some sleep at the top before the sun came up.

Thanking the owner of the taverna for the sumptuous meal, the group shouldered their packs and left the restaurant to his wishes of *sto kalo* in their ears. Although the moon was almost full and the group were wearing head torches, the wisdom of taking a guide was apparent when, not long after beginning the climb, they reached a chapel and had to leave the path they had been following, which Nikos told them led to the Idean Cave. In the dark, Amy was sure they would have missed the small red arrows and yellow markers which pointed the way up the mountain.

They were now joining a small section of the E4 walking trail which crossed Europe, beginning in Spain. The Cretan leg of the path began in the northwest of the island in Kastelli Kissamou and relentlessly scaled the mountains that ran across the heart of the island before reaching the coast again in Kato Zakros in the east. Hearing about the trail, Andrew's ears pricked up and he seemed eager to learn more from Nikos. Amy listened as their guide answered her friend's enthusiastic questions. To do the whole walk along the spine of Crete would take a strong walker the best part of a month, and it would be important to choose the time of year wisely. In high summer the days were too hot to take on the arduous climbs and in winter the snow made the high mountain passes inaccessible.

Amy was finding the part of the trail they had just embarked on challenging enough, and could not imagine walking the whole way across the island. She found her own pace and left Andrew, Emma and Nikos to lead as she fell in with Suzi and Stelios and felt reassurance walking with the doctor and his wife. As they walked, Amy listened to Suzi explaining to her husband about the various names held by Crete's tallest mountain. Psiloritis, meaning 'tall mountain', usually referred to the range but its older name of Mount Ida was thought to stem from the word 'da', meaning 'mother of all gods'. This, Suzi believed, was connected to Rhea, the mother of Zeus and the location of the Idean Cave nestling on the mountainside. The peak itself was known by locals as Timios Stavros, after the chapel of the Holy Cross standing there.

Nikos regularly stopped so the dispersed group could come back together. In the darkness it would have been all too easy for them to lose their way, particularly when looking down to avoid turning an ankle on the rugged track. Amy was grateful for the frequent rests and each time rummaged in her pack for the chocolate she had brought to give her energy. She had with her a good supply, and was pleased she had, as it was dwindling. She thought how at one time she would have taken the lead, but now she was content to follow the others in the company of Stelios and Suzi. Her friends were happy to stop whenever Amy needed to catch her breath. She was grateful for Stelios' whispered enquiries about how she was coping and laughingly assured him she had never felt happier.

Although warm in the clothes she wore, Amy could feel the cold on her face as they got higher and pulled her woollen hat down further over her ears. There was less talking among the group now. Whether it was because of the toll the climb was taking on their energy or that the rest of the group shared in the reverie, Amy felt that she was on the verge of witnessing something astounding. As the group grew quieter, Amy became more aware of the lilting ring of goats' bells floating up the mountain from their pastures in the foothills.

Ahead, the climbers could see the snow line. Nikos stopped to reassure them that they would be safe as long as they followed him and took care where they stepped. The ground crackled underfoot as the group left their footprints in the snow. Amy could sense the mountain dropping away on either side of her and realised just how far they had come. In front of her for the first time she could make out the shadow of the peak. She estimated that it would be less than half an hour before they reached the culmination of their trek.

In silence the group climbed onto the flat plateau of rock which marked the end of their ascent. It was still dark, but the milky light of dawn began to mix with the night sky. Looking out, Amy could see cloud beneath her, through which she knew lay the whole of the island she had loved since she first set foot there thirty years earlier.

With less than an hour until daylight, Nikos suggested they rest before the sun came up as he wanted to make the descent in the cool of the morning. Amy turned away from the void and wondered at the devotion of those who had built the small stone chapel. She could see the crude frame of a belfry and in the light of her head torch made out a sign reading 'Timios Stavros 2456m'. Finding the entrance to the church, she went in and was surprised to see the flickering of lit candles illuminating icons propped up against the bare stone walls. She shivered and went back outside. Some of the others were bedding down to rest and await the dawn. Amy reached into her backpack for her sleeping bag, found a not too rocky spot in the crook of the chapel wall and zipped her bed up around her. She looked up at the stars, their light about to give way to the dawn of the new day, and fell asleep.

When Emma couldn't rouse her sister, her shrieks of anguish echoed around the surrounding peaks. Stelios came running, kneeling down beside where Amy lay. As the sobs pulsed through her, with every tear that fell, any hope Emma had for the future lay with them on the frozen ground.

*

Life appeared to go into slow motion for Emma as the fear gripped her. She stood on the mountaintop in shock as Stelios worked on trying to revive her sister. She barely noticed Andrew as he put a comforting arm around her shoulders and tried to steer her away from where her sister lay motionless.

It seemed an eternity before they heard the news they feared they might never hear. Stelios had managed to restart Amy's failing heart. Nikos took a thermal blanket from his pack and covered Amy in it before laying another sleeping bag over her to keep her warm. All the while Stelios knelt beside her, talking to keep her conscious.

The sound of the rescue helicopter came as some relief to Emma but she was distraught that she couldn't accompany her sister and Stelios as she was airlifted to hospital in Heraklion. The anxious wait for news as the group followed Nikos down the mountainside filled Emma with torment. She was aware that Andrew had tried to comfort her, but in the moment she was struck by fear at the thought of losing her sister and had shrugged him off. As they traipsed further downhill, Emma became more and more withdrawn as the anxiety in her grew.

The group were halfway through their descent of Psiloritis when Stelios called Suzi, who passed her phone to Emma. He reassured her that Amy was stable but was having an emergency operation to have a pacemaker fitted to keep her heart beating regularly. Despite Stelios' reassurances, Emma could not rid herself of her fears. She wondered if Stelios had known that her sister's heart was weak, and if so, why had he let her climb the mountain?

Emma refused Andrew's offer to stay with her after he dropped her off at the hospital in Heraklion. Even on seeing her sister awake and Stelios insisting that she would be alright, she could not shake off the dread of what might have been. While her sister recovered over the next days, Emma stayed at her bedside, only leaving the ward to get food for them both.

It was only three days later that Amy was discharged. Stelios came to drive them home to the village and he was delighted to see his friend, whom he had brought back to life on the summit of Mount Ida, looking so well, smiling and laughing. He was more worried about Emma who looked tired and was withdrawn, barely speaking throughout the hour-long drive.

Before her sister's heart attack, Emma had felt happier than she could remember for a long time, and was pleased to let life take her where it would. Now the path ahead of her looked dark and she couldn't see a way through. She determined that she would stay with her sister and look after her. Emma was frightened that without Amy, she would be left alone. She told herself that she was being selfish, but nothing she did could still the anguish that she felt. The shock of nearly losing Amy had thrown her into a chasm of depression out of which she couldn't climb.

Alice tried to comfort her mother when she had called to tell her the news of what had happened, but with her preparing for her finals in England, before no doubt embarking on a career in the City, she was unable to fly out to Crete.

Amy had recovered well from the operation and, with the pacemaker fitted, if anything felt better than she had for some time. Within a week she was keen to get back to her painting and although she appreciated Emma's concern for her wellbeing she felt smothered by her sister's constant attention. Since that day on the mountain, Emma had hardly left Amy's side. She no longer spent time with Andrew, and Amy noticed her sister sliding back into the depression she had experienced following their mother's death and the breakdown of her marriage.

Not only was Amy concerned for her sister's welfare, but she found her constant attention stifling. The only time she got to herself was when she managed to persuade Emma to go to Elounda to pick up some shopping, and even then she took the jeep and was back as quickly as possible.

Stelios came to visit every couple of days to check on his friend's progress, and most days Andrew would pop in to see how she was getting on, although Amy suspected he also wanted to check on her sister. If that were the case he was only to be disappointed, as Emma would shrink into herself and would barely utter a word to the neighbour who just weeks before she had been so close to.

Both Amy and Andrew wanted to do something to restore Emma's equilibrium. Amy understood that it was a deep-seated fear of losing her after their reconciliation which was at the root of Emma's anxiety. Before the trek up the mountain, she had thought that her sister may have been falling for Andrew but now she shied away from any contact with him. Alongside her fear of her sister dying, Emma was also afraid of forming a relationship with anyone else.

Andrew was distraught. The affection he felt for Emma had crept up on him and he had hoped that their friendship might turn into something deeper. One day when Emma had left the house to go shopping, he opened up to Amy about his feelings. Amy also worried about her neighbour regressing into the depression he too had been in following the death of Isabelle. Both Emma and Andrew had suffered grief in their own ways.

'Why don't you take some time out and do that walk across Crete?' Amy didn't know where the suggestion had come from. 'You could ask Emma to go with you. If she agrees, it will do you both good. If not, absence may make the heart grow fonder, and at least it will give you a break from the situation.'

At first Andrew was reluctant to leave Emma for the hike but as the days went by he could see that her mood was not lightening and that maybe his presence was hindering her battle with anxiety. He would ask her to come with him as Amy had suggested. If she refused there was little he could do and he would go alone.

Amy was desperate to get out of the house and to see her friends in the taverna. She knew that Emma would be reluctant but would not like Amy to go alone. If Amy insisted on going out, it might make Emma confront her fears. One Sunday lunchtime, Amy announced she had organised to meet with the walking society. Emma, after protesting, realised that she was adamant.

Inside, the taverna was bustling. It was the first time Amy had been in since she had fallen ill on the mountain and her friends and other villagers were keen to show their concern. As they gathered round to talk to Amy, Emma felt her isolation keenly. She was sitting beneath an open window, but the slight breeze did little to cool her face which had broken into a sweat. She felt the beads of perspiration on her forehead and a shiver inside. She rose and made for the door, almost falling into the lane outside.

'Are you OK?' She heard Stelios beside her.

'I'll be fine. I just need to get some air. I want to be on my own for a bit.' At her response the doctor reluctantly stopped and let Emma walk away. She allowed the paths to take her where they would, but she could not clear the maelstrom which raged in her head.

At the end of a narrow path she came across a chapel. Rounding its walls she found herself in a dusty courtyard, a stone wall holding back the terrace from falling down the mountainside. In the heat her head span and she sat down on the wall. Blinking in the sunlight, she tried to focus on the olive groves that rippled down the slopes to the bay below. Through the rasping of cicadas, from somewhere she heard the long melancholy note which stirred something in her memory. The sound of a lyra playing.

'May I?' At the sound of a familiar voice Emma looked up. Coming closer, Andrew sat beside her on the wall.

'This probably won't help at the moment, but I'll say it anyway. I know how you feel. When Isabelle died I was lost and angry. I couldn't see a way forward. Your sister, her love and the way she encouraged me to build the garden has helped me through that. Then along came you to help rebuild my house and make it a home again. Of course, I am still sad. Of course, I still love Isabelle and always will. But I see a life in front of me.

'Isabelle loved life. She always said, "Don't be so afraid of dying that you are too scared to live." She loved life and lived it to the full.' Andrew hesitated. 'There's something I want to ask you.'

Emma looked up into the eyes of the man who just weeks before she had thought she was falling for. Now her emotions were so dulled she felt devoid of everything but a clawing depression.

'Will you come away with me?' Emma was unsure what Andrew was asking. 'For some time I've been planning to walk the length of Crete from east to west. I wanted to ask you before but I never quite found the right moment.'

Emma sat in silence. Andrew registered the shock on her face.

'Why would I want to do that?' she responded, standing. 'I think I'd better get back to the taverna.'

Andrew could see there would be no reasoning with her. Inwardly he chided himself for the way he had approached the subject. He could see there was no point in going after her. During the climb on Psiloritis he had thought they were getting closer. By inviting her to join him on his epic trek he'd hoped it might divert her from her anxiety. He now knew that this had been stupid. In his haste he had probably lost her forever.

It had been his intention to leave on the walk as soon as possible, but he decided to put off his departure. After all the help she had given him, he owed Emma all the support he could give her.

From where she now sat in the taverna, Emma watched as Andrew walked past, his shoulders dropped. He did not come in. Her eyes followed him up the lane as he walked in the direction of his house. She hated herself for pushing him away but for some reason was too afraid to get close to another person. She was better off on her own. That way she would not be hurt again.

*

Throughout the following weeks, Andrew's attempts to connect with Emma were met with a dispassion which pained him deeply. Talking to her proved to be impossible; when he called at Amy's house, his attempts to rekindle their friendship were met with stony indifference. Andrew could feel himself sinking back into sadness and despair. He had done all he could to get through to Emma but needed to get away or he would return to the black place he had been in following Isabelle's death.

One morning, Andrew slung his rucksack across his shoulders, called Bella and slipped a lead around her before closing the front door on his house. Stelios and Suzi had offered to give him a lift to Kato Zakros, a seaside village in the far east of the island. He had booked into a beachfront pension from where he would begin his trek the next day. Although Amy knew of his intention to leave soon, he had not told her of his imminent departure.

Quite how long the epic walk following the island's section of the European Hiking Route would take him, he did not know. He had measured the trek as being approximately 200 miles but it traversed the four towering mountain ranges of Thripti, Dhikti, Psiloritis and the Lefka Ori before winding its way along the west coast. He had hoped Emma might join him and that their relationship might flourish on the shared adventure. Springing the idea on her had been stupid, but now more than ever he needed to escape the village and come to terms with where his life was taking him. Now he needed the solitude of the trek to be alone with his thoughts.

As Stelios confidently drove the road that clung to the rocks, they asked if he hadn't thought of asking a friend to join him. When Suzi voiced the idea that it may have done Emma some good to have accompanied him, she immediately knew she had hit a raw nerve. 'I tried, but she said no', was his only response. Suzi, concerned that she had upset their friend tried to coax Andrew to talk about his feelings and he gradually opened up about his affection for Emma and his thoughtless miscalculation.

From behind him he felt the cold, wet nose of Bella on the back of his neck and turned to pat her head, taking consolation in the knowledge that she would still be with him. The road descended steeply, and between the hairpin bends the town of Sitia was laid out before them. Navigating the busy streets they took the road which followed the coast before heading inland to Palekastro and south to their destination of Kato Zakros. Finding his room, Andrew deposited his rucksack before heading to a waterfront taverna with his friends for lunch before their drive back to the village.

That morning when Emma awoke she felt a pang of loneliness she couldn't shake. She made a coffee and took it onto the terrace. She stared out on the landscape but nothing could lighten her mood. She knew she had been unfair to Andrew and that she had pushed him away when he was trying to show her kindness. She knew he was in torment, but her fear of getting hurt and leaving her sister alone had brought down an impregnable barrier between them. As she'd driven Andrew further away from her and as the chasm between them grew, the more in her heart Emma had regretted it.

Was her fear of what might happen in the future worse than the pain she was now feeling?

'You're up early.' Amy emerged onto the terrace, stretching.

'I've been stupid, haven't I?' Emma turned towards her sister and her face crumbled.

'You know, I really can cope on my own, and I have lots of friends in the village if I need anything.' Amy laid a hand on Emma's shoulder. 'It may or may not work out, but who's to say if you don't give it a try? Why don't you go and tell him, I really do need to go into Agios Nikolaos today for some art supplies and I'd like to try going on my own.'

Pushing open the gate, Emma walked across the terrace and bent to avoid a stray shoot hanging from a shrub which bordered the path. Knocking on the door, she pushed. It was locked. There was no sound of barking and the windows were shuttered. She was too late. Why had she been so foolish?

Emma sat on the wall, contemplating the time she had spent on Crete since her mother's death. Had she not been happier here than she had at any time since childhood? That night on the mountain, she knew she was falling for Andrew and before her sister's heart attack she had decided to take that leap of faith.

She walked back to Amy's house and climbed the stairs to the studio, browsing through the paintings stacked against the walls. She began to pick up brushes and palette knives, stacking them in the pottery jugs her sister had used for storage. She collected the half-squeezed tubes of paint and began arranging them into colours. Stopping herself, she gathered the tubes and put them in plastic storage boxes. She then washed all the surfaces, before cleaning the bare wooden floor.

With the studio in some sort of order, Emma looked around her. The room, now tidy, had lost something of the soul of her sister. Distraught, she began to take brushes and knives from the jugs and paint from the boxes and redistribute them around the room. She found herself perspiring and her breath quickening. Feeling faint she stepped outside and with some effort forced herself to breathe more deeply. She stepped towards the wall, fighting the vertigo her anxiety had induced. She bent down and reached for a chair, pulling it across the tiles so she could sit.

It was late afternoon when she heard the front door open but couldn't find the courage to stand up. Amy, sensing something was wrong, put down her shopping bags and ran to where Emma sat rooted to the chair, her hands tightly gripping the seat. Bending down she hugged her sister and held her tight. She could feel her short, quick breaths on her chest and rubbed her back to slow down her breathing. Slowly Emma relaxed her grip on the chair and her body went limp. She held Amy tight for fear of collapsing and gave way to her emotions.

She did not know where it came from but Emma poured out her feelings about how she had felt as a child when Amy had stayed out in Crete and she had had to deal with the fallout from the breakup of their parents' marriage. How somewhere along the line she had lost her way and fallen into marriage to a man who had controlled her and how, now that Alice was about to finish university, she would lose her to the big wide world. She cried as she told Amy how scared she had been that she had died on the mountain and now they had rekindled their relationship it might be snatched away from them again.

Amy let Emma vent her frustrations and fears before trying to comfort her. She reassured her sister that the doctors had claimed that she was fully recovered now she had a pacemaker fitted, and that Emma was welcome to stay with her for as long as she wanted. She reminded Emma of Christmas and how much Alice had enjoyed spending time with her mother. And, as for her marriage, wasn't she better off out of it? She reminded her that she had friends in the village and was not alone.

'Are you there?' The voice of Suzi calling up from the alley below interrupted them.

Emma's vertigo had passed, and the two women looked down over the wall to see Suzi and Stelios staring up.

'We were just going to the taverna for a drink and wondered if you wanted to join us?' Suzi asked.

Amy looked towards her sister and whispered, 'Shall we?'

Emma nodded.

'Yes, we'd like that. Can we meet you there in twenty minutes, I need to change?' Amy replied to their friends, knowing Emma would want to take some time to compose herself, wash her face and put on some make-up.

In the familiar surroundings of Alexander's taverna, Stelios told them how they had driven Andrew and Bella to Kato Zakros. Emma admitted she had gone to see Andrew earlier in the day but that he had already left.

'Have I made a big mistake?'

Amy, Suzi and Stelios said nothing but Emma could see the answer on their faces and heard it in their silence.

'It's not too late,' said Suzi, looking at her husband.

'Come on, I'll help you get some things together.' Amy stood, pulling her sister out of the taverna and back to the house almost before Emma realised what was happening.

*

In the darkness, Stelios eased the car around the hairpin bends. On one side, they sensed the oily sea below and on the other the mountains towering above them. When Suzi and Stelios realised Emma's change of heart they offered to retrace their earlier journey, trying to reach Andrew before his early start from the pension the next morning.

Amy had helped Emma hastily stuff a rucksack with a sleeping bag, some clothes and a wash bag before the two of them joined Suzi and Stelios where their car was parked beside the church. In the dark the drive would take some time, but Stelios insisted that he could get to the far east of the island by daybreak.

As Stelios flicked the main beam on and off, Emma caught glimpses of the rugged landscape. Sometimes they revealed darkness reaching out to infinity, others an imposing wall of rock looming above them. Closing her eyes, she allowed herself to drift into the security of sleep, her head rested on Amy's shoulder.

Woken by the milky colour wash of the early morning light, Emma blinked and looked out at the sun rising from the calm of the waters ahead as the car descended towards the sea. For a moment as the cool light of the new day permeated the last vestiges of night she felt herself quiver. Was she doing the right thing? The sun rose in the sky, clearing it to blue as a slight breeze ruffled the sea beneath them. Stelios brought the car to a halt, getting out of the vehicle and stretching.

Shouldering his pack, Andrew descended the steps from the pension. He almost stumbled as Bella pulled on the lead letting out a bark.

'I think you've forgotten something.' At Amy's voice he looked across and saw her getting out of the car before the back door opened. Emma pulled out her pack. A smile spread wide across Andrew's face.

'I'd like to join you. If you'll still have me?'

Epilogue

2022

EMMA RADIATED PRIDE as she looked across the terrace of The Boatyard taverna. She could sense the nerves in Alice as she set up on the stage beside a relaxed Phoebe and her friend Sarah. She could hear the animation in Andrew's voice as he stood chatting to friends at another table.

Emma looked out along a jetty at the end of which a caique sat berthed, gently swaying. Across the bay the evening light picked out the colours on the dusty island beyond, brown, yellow and green.

When she had set off with Andrew on their hike across the island, she had not known what the future held. But in her wildest dreams she could never imagine the happiness she now felt. She knew it would not always be like this, but for now she savoured the elation inside her.

She thought back to how the walk had challenged and changed her in so many ways. It had been tough at first, but they had taken their time. Day by day her love for Andrew had grown. Their bodies got lean and fit and the freedom of the mountains provided the space for their souls to breathe and heal. Neither of them could forget the past, but with every mile they walked they could enjoy the beauty that was around them and a path into the future opened up.

On their return after more than a month of walking, Emma had been delighted to hear that Alice, having graduated from university, was coming to Crete. Emma had moved in with Andrew, and Amy had suggested that Alice could live with her. The first evening of her visit, Alice had announced that she had given up on a career in business and wanted to pursue her ambition to be a musician. Since she had returned to university from Crete at Christmas, she told them she had spent more time practicing the guitar and piano than working for her finals. She knew that music made her happy and fulfilled, and as she had grown further away from her father's influence she had found the strength to plot her own course in life.

Andrew had already begun to write his novel and Emma had also embarked on an account of their trek through the mountains. They would both start work early in the day, Emma taking her laptop to the front terrace overlooking the bay, whilst Andrew wrote on the terrace under the pergola. Bella would spend some time with each of them before the sun grew too hot and she would settle in the shade of the fruit trees on the path.

Sometimes Emma could hear the strains of music drifting on the breeze from the house next door. She would stop her writing and listen. There was no doubt her daughter had talent and she was pleased that Alice had chosen to pursue her love of music. The thought was tinged with regret that she had not followed her own dream of writing a book sooner but then realised that if life had taken that course it would not have brought her to the contentment she now had.

The taverna was quickly filling up. Many of the villagers had walked down the mountain path to spend the evening. Passing tourists, seeing how full the terrace was, had decided to eat there. Emma and Andrew had taken a table with their friends from the walking society. The conversation was of shared experiences or the many hikes they had taken and Emma realised she was now able to talk about the trek up Psiloritis without the memory taking her to a dark place.

The table fell silent as a single note emanated from the stage. It seemed to surpass the length of the bow Sarah drew across the strings of the instrument balanced on her knee. As the sound flew away across the bay and echoed around the hills beyond it was joined by the guitars of Phoebe and Alice winding a mellow melody around the stark music of the lyra.

Looking up at Alice, through the concentration Emma could see the joy on her face. She was born to do this. The music the women played infected the whole room, and at the end of each song the crowd clapped and shouted. When the musicians stopped for a break, Alice joined her mother at the table. Flushed with the success of her performance and the adrenalin which coursed through her body, Alice threw her arms around her mother and kissed her. Emma had been meaning to tell her daughter the news after the performance but in the emotion of the moment could not resist telling her that her grandmother's estate had finally been settled and that as neither she nor Amy were in need of money they had decided to give it to Alice.

It was easily enough to secure Alice's future. If she thought she could not be happier, Alice's heart was now brimming with elation. This would let her continue making the music she loved, and to be near her mother. She was still crying with joy as she returned to the stage. The rapture Alice felt suffused the music and the space in front of the musicians was soon taken up by dancers, the line twisting its way around the tables and spilling out onto road and the beach beyond. Andrew stood up to dance and was soon joined by Amy and the other friends from the walking group.

Alone at the table, Emma thought of the events that had bought her here. She raised her glass and drank a silent toast to Alice, Amy, Andrew and her friends in the village walking society.

Did You Enjoy this Book?

If you liked reading this book and have time, any review on www.amazon.co.uk or www.amazon.com would be appreciated. My website *Notes from Greece* is https://notesfromgreece.com, and it would be good to meet up with any readers on my facebook page at www.facebook.com/richardclarkbooks.

Printed in Great Britain
by Amazon